THE BEAST

LIKE ME

The WOLVES of WHARTON
Book Six

THE BEAST
LIKE ME

BEAU LAKE

4 Horsemen
Publications, Inc.

4 Horsemen
Publications, Inc.

4 Horsemen Publications, Inc.
1497 Main St. Suite 169
Dunedin, FL 34698
4horsemenpublications.com
info@4horsemenpublications.com

Cover by 4 Horsemen Publications, Inc.
Typesetting by Autumn Skye
Editor Laura Mita

Library of Congress Control Number: 2022936844

Print ISBN: 978-1-64450-613-4
Audio ISBN: 978-1-64450-611-0
Ebook ISBN: 978-1-64450-612-7

DEDICATION

For M, para siempre.

ACKNOWLEDGMENTS

———◁◆▷———

Thank you to my family and friends, for their unyielding support.

Thank you to the Horsemen, for believing in me and this series.

Thank you, reader.

I'll see you again in New York, in a little neighborhood called West Egg. I can hear the jazz music already...

TABLE OF CONTENTS

PROLOGUE

––––––◁◆▷––––––

Sevierville, Tennessee—August 1970

I t is muggy in the hayloft. Sweat prickles upon my brow and dribbles into my eyes. It stings just like swimming without goggles in the Sevier County pool, the chlorine staining the sclera pink. I wipe my face dry with my shirt tail before lying amidst the loose hay.

The rifle is too big in my hands, the pommel butting uncomfortably against my shoulder. I squint through the scope, the crosshairs strafing across the farmyard. The chickens are loose, pecking at the dry, pockmarked earth. The rooster's crimson comb bobs as he meanders around the yard like a southern dandy strolling a balustrade. With the scope, I can see his big, unblinking eye. "Bang," I whisper, imagining the bullet shredding his pea-sized brain. *That'll teach you to chase me 'round the yard, Drumstick.*

The strands of loose alfalfa stab at my bare skin. I find myself wondering why they call you-know-what a "roll in the hay." I suppose the phrase is meant to be titillating, reminiscent of a clandestine affair. But perhaps it is meant to invoke the fragility of one's skin, its penchant for tearing.

Dust flurries in the hayloft, sticking to my eyelashes. I don't dare blink.

There's movement in the kitchen window. I swing the rifle's barrel toward the cheery gingham curtains, and I find my mother at the sink with foamy suds up to her elbows. She's cleaning up from lunch: egg salad sandwiches, the yolk a silky, fluorescent yellow. When I exhale, I can still smell the mayonnaise on my breath. There's a faint vinegary note that reminds me of decorating Easter eggs, the pastel dye staining my fingertips for days afterward. I am too far away to hear her, but I know she is humming; she loves to sing along to the radio but can never remember the words.

I jerk the crosshairs away from her freckled skin and pursed lips; seeing her through the scope gives me a queasy feeling. Or is that the mayo, curdling in my stomach? "Focus, Henry!" I grumble through gritted teeth. *You have a divine mission, given to you by God, the Father—and your father, too.*

My eyes water, tears streaming down my cheeks. I allow myself one blink, hissing as dust stings my eyes. I carefully put down the gun, swiping at my grubby face with the tail of my Memphis Tigers t-shirt. "Dang!"

At the curse, I slap my hands over my mouth. There's no one to hear, but God heard, didn't he? I imagine Him lying beside me in the hay, his sandaled feet swinging and his bearded chin resting on his knuckles. *Whatcha thinkin' about, Henry Lee? Are you thinkin' about me? Tee-hee!*

Fo-CUS!

In the barn below, the cow, Evangeline, bumps her feed bucket, scattering pellets. The metallic clang of the handle startles me, and I yelp. Peering down the ladder to make sure I am alone, I spot only the cow's refrigerator-shaped body, fanning away flies with her ears. Unperturbed by the mess, she simply bows her head, lapping the pellets up with her thick pink tongue.

I pick up the rifle from the straw, cradling it in my arms. Despite the heat, the metal is still cold.

Outside, the screen door slams. Samuel Campbell coughs. His boots clomp on the porch as he hustles toward the yard, an oversized bag of feed balanced on his shoulder. The chickens hop around my stepfather's feet, and he gently nudges them out of his way with his toe. Agitated, Drumstick flaps his wings, the hackle feathers around his thin neck puffing out.

"Don't you dare," Samuel warns the rooster, "or you'll be baked and stuffed with mushrooms come dinnertime."

I hurriedly raise the rifle, squinting through the scope. The heavy weapon bucks in my trembling hands, the edge of the scope butting painfully against my brow bone. Surely, it will leave a bruise. The scope magnifies the feed bag's label. It's brightly colored with chubby cartoon pigs sitting at a table, holding a fork in one cloven hoof and a knife in the other. They are violently pink and wearing gingham bandanas tucked beneath their fat, bristly chins. Samuel is heading toward the potbellied pigs' pasture just beyond the barn.

He pauses, readjusting the bag on his shoulder. I can see his face now: sun-reddened, weathered, tendrils of dark hair clinging to his sweat-soaked brow. He's wearing a Sevierville Swallowtail baseball cap, the brim sun-faded and battered. He came to every one of my games this season, sitting wide-legged on the bleachers, crushing that hat in his calloused hands every time I came up to bat ("Let's go, Hen-ree!").

I can't do this.

My stomach churns, hot bile sloshing up into my throat. I burp, the taste of stomach acid settling onto my tongue. I try to spit, but the sputum seems to cling to my uvula. Gagging, a foamy trickle of slaver edges down my chin. I don't wipe it away, afraid that if I put down the rifle I won't be able to pick it up again. Surely, it will weigh more than Sisyphus' boulder.

"Even Satan disguises himself as an angel of light," I recite under my breath, rolling my stiff shoulders. "His servants, also, disguise themselves as servants of right-right-righteousness." I stumble over the last word. I don't quite know what it means, but Father Ricci reads it with the same breathless reverence he has for Jesus Christ and the Holy Ghost. Or when my pal Eddie gushes about Mary Ann from *Gilligan's Island*.

"Where's Henry?" Samuel calls as my mother steps out onto the porch, hanging tea towels on the rail to dry. Through the scope, I spot the one I sloppily embroidered in home economics, the stitching loose. It's meant to be a dancing duck, but it looks more like a goose that has been flattened by a speeding car.

"He's in the barn, I think," she says.

Samuel turns toward the barn and, inexplicably, up at the hay door beneath the gambrel roof. It's as though he felt my eyes on him. He pales when he spots me there: his thirteen-year-old gangly-limbed stepson holding a rifle. When our eyes lock through the scope's lens, I curl my finger around the trigger. Just as I squeeze it, Samuel drops the heavy feed bag.

Bang! The bullet punches through the bag, pellets bouncing around the yard like shrapnel. The chickens scatter, shedding feathers on the brown grass. It should have killed Samuel, but he isn't there anymore. There's only a long divot in the dirt. I think my mother is screaming, but I can't hear her over the ringing in my ears. I can only see her wide mouth, her eyes bulging from their sockets, her hands clutching the porch rail so hard I can see bone.

Suddenly, a massive paw grasps the hayloft's ledge, the claws pulverizing the wood. They are long and sharp, not all that dissimilar from the grizzly bear claw I got to hold at the Boy Scout jamboree last autumn. A hulking creature pulls itself up into the loft, its growls reverberating through my body like my cat's purrs when she lays upon my chest. The beast looks like an enormous wolf albeit bipedal, with sinuous muscles and a wiry coat. Globules of saliva drip off of its teeth as it edges toward me, careful to avoid the molding floorboard. Just the night before, Samuel reminded me that we had to replace it before one of us fell into Evangeline's stall.

There was a full moon last night, did you know that?

I aim the gun and squeeze the trigger, but the bullet doesn't hit the beast. Instead, a hole opens in the roof, a handful of copper tiles skittering down the side of the barn. Evangeline moos, throwing her shoulder against her stall door. When it doesn't give, she throws herself at the opposite wall, shaking the whole barn. Or are those my knees rattling?

The beast bends the gun's barrel as though it's as malleable as play-doh. I can't help but think of Bugs Bunny tying Elmer Fudd's gun into a perfect bow. I stare at the bent metal, the beast's fist still gripping the muzzle. I smell burnt fur, acrid and sulfurous. I'm fairly certain it's what hell smells like.

"Stupid boy," the beast growls in my stepfather's voice, wrenching the gun from my quivering hands. "Who put you up to this?"

I. November

CHAPTER 1
(HUNTER)

————◁◆▷————

I sit on the stairs just beyond the reach of the porchlight. The sand is still warm from the autumnal sun,
and I take my shoes and socks off to plunge my toes
into it. Voices sieve through the screen door behind
me, but I can hardly hear them over the breakers
crashing upon the tetrapods. The three-quarter moon
hangs low on the horizon, spilling silvery light upon
the sand. Ghost crabs, housed in their pearly shells,
skitter across the shoreline, foraging for tasty coquina
clams to nibble on. As children, Candy and I loved
to hunt ghost crabs, trapping them in the beam of our
flashlights.

Inside, someone howls. It's an ostensibly human
sound: a lark, nothing more. Still, I find myself cringing
away, wrapping my arms around my knees. I had to
excuse myself, not wanting to hear one more word
about prey or pack politics. The wolves become raucous when they are together, especially when alcohol

is plentiful. I consider feigning illness, but I know Angus will give me *that look*. It's the same look he gives me when I avoid his kisses, offering him only the stubbly plane of my jaw rather than my lips. We've hardly touched in months.

The screen door opens, crashing upon its hinges. I don't have to turn around to know it's Angus; he walks with the heavy stride of a Percheron in a parade. "Dinner is ready," he announces, his voice a little thick from the Pinot Grigio.

"I'll be there in a few minutes," I murmur, wiggling my toes in the sand.

Angus comes to sit beside me, his rounded hip butting against mine. He's wearing a pair of chinos, a narrow leather belt threaded through the loops. It looks as though he's been poured into them. "Are you alright?" he asks, draping an arm around my narrow shoulders.

"Should I be?" I ask, my eyes on the ocean.

Angus sighs, running his free hand through his glossy hair. I wonder if it's exhausting—being with me. Is he tired of having this same conversation over and over? I wipe at my dry eyes with the heel of my hand, sucking my lower lip between my teeth.

"It's *Thanksgiving*, Hunt. Can we please not do this tonight?" he asks.

"I'm not doing anything," I counter. "I'm just sitting."

Angus' arm drops off my shoulders, slapping against the wooden floorboards. The hollow sound makes me flinch. "Ama wants to say grace," he grumbles. "It'll be rude not to be sitting at the table when she does. C'mon." He rises, sticking his hand out to haul me to my feet. I reluctantly reach for it.

"Hunter—"

"Hmm?" I busy myself brushing sand off the soles of my feet, gripping his forearm to keep from toppling over. I slip my feet into my fawn-colored boat shoes, keenly aware of the grit I wasn't able to sweep off.

Angus gently cups my chin, tilting my head toward his. For a moment, I think he intends to kiss me, but he's frowning. His mouth doesn't quite cooperate; the gully traversing his cheek is thick with waxy, pinkish scar tissue, dragging the corner of his lip up. It makes him appear perpetually besotted. He's wearing the leather eyepatch Toby crafted for him, the braided strap skimming his eyebrow. He hasn't been fitted for a prosthetic yet, but I know an artist will never be able to capture the brilliant blue of his iris—the exact color of the ocean when the sun is at its apex. "Why won't you talk to me?" he asks.

"Ama wants to say grace," I remind him sweetly. Before he can protest, I trot up the stairs, tripping on the uneven step. Angus follows, catching the screen door before it can slam shut in my wake.

The living room furniture has been pushed up against the walls, leaving space for three card tables set end-to-end, shrouded in a linen tablecloth. The chairs are a collection of cast-offs, including two stools, four straight-backed chairs with upholstered cushions, and one rocking chair. Much like everything in the bungalow, the tablecloth hails from some bygone era; the hem is so tattered it resembles fringe. Still, the pattern is festive: hand-painted cornucopias laden with brightly colored gourds, bundles of dried wheat stalks, and fruit; leaves in red and gold; and cartoonish turkeys wearing buckled capotains. The table has been set since I excused myself, the dinnerware mismatched. Dainty crystal stemware is coupled with Pyrex plates in an unsightly saffron, silverware flanking every place setting. No two pieces of cutlery are from the same set.

Ama Chilton sits at the head of the table, dressed in a boat-necked sweater and tapered cigarette pants. Three strands of pearls adorn her throat. Even in her nineties, she looks like a cover model. I can almost picture her as she once was: dark pin curls, red lipstick, and eyes as blue as a robin's egg. The chair to her right is empty, reserved for her grandson. Angus brushes past me, giving her bony hand an affectionate squeeze. Even enveloped in his massive paw, the tremor in her hands is apparent. We are all careful not to draw attention to it; it's impolite.

I pull out the vacant chair between Angus and my sister, Candy, draping my coat over it. Haley, perched on the stool opposite, tips her glass back, swallowing the dregs of her cocktail. She fishes the wedge of lime out of the glass with her fingers, sucking the gin-infused juice from the fruit until the flesh turns wrinkly. "Are you okay?" she asks, raising her eyebrows. A trickle of liquid edges down her wrist, but she doesn't seem to notice.

I shrug, dragging my linen napkin into my lap.

Candy glances from her girlfriend to me. "What's going on?" she whispers.

"Nothing," I mutter, indignant. "I was just taking a breather outside. I wasn't aware that it would cause an international incident." I can feel Angus stiffen next to me, but he continues speaking animatedly to his grandmother as if he hadn't heard at all.

Alexandre pushes open the kitchen door with his shoulder, carrying the main course upon a silver-plated serving tray. The whole turkey is roasted to perfection, its golden skin still sizzling from the oven. Sprigs of fragrant rosemary garnish the bird, and aromatic stuffing—cubed bread, carrots, onions, and mushrooms—spills out of its chest cavity. It's a large turkey; Alexandre's ropy forearms bulge under the weight.

Her round belly leading the way, Toby follows with a basket of flaky croissants in one hand and a serving dish of mashed potatoes in the other. Haley bolts to help her, almost toppling her chair.

Once the spread is placed on the table, Alexandre sits on Ama's left, and Toby takes the chair beside Haley. Ama clears her throat. When she smiles, the tissue-thin skin of her eyelids crinkles. "Before we enjoy this lovely meal, I would like to say grace," she says. While old age shrinks her, bending her in half like a bonsai tree, her voice is clear and emphatic. "I'm not one who holds much stock in religion, or even God, but there's something to be said about expressing thanks for a meal—imbuing it with power." She folds her hands upon the tabletop and bows her head. "Thank you to Alexandre for cooking this beautiful bird."

The Frenchman blushes a violent shade of crimson. "Bon appétit," he murmurs. "Je suis honoré, Ama."

"Thank you to my grandson, Angus, for bringing a pack to me. I hadn't realized how lonely I was until my house was filled with noise again. Soon, we will even be blessed with the pitter-patter of tiny paws."

"Not soon enough!" Toby interjects, patting her stomach.

"We have suffered a tremendous loss this year. Renner should be sitting at this table tonight," Ama continues. Her cerulean eyes rest on the empty chair at the far end of the table, her lip quivering just slightly. I find myself staring at the chair too as if expecting to see the foul-mouthed fisherman materialize there. But it's just an empty chair, a bit of yellowed stuffing peeking out of the seam.

"But I think, tonight, that we should focus on our perseverance," she continues, "and what we have gained—"

I laugh. I can't hold it in; it punches its way out, doubling me over. At first, it's just a guffaw—a shriek, really. Then I dissolve into humorless giggles. "I'm sorry," I gasp, wiping tears from my cheeks. "I'm really sorry. That's just a very funny way to put it. 'Our perseverance?' All I see is floundering. Take Haley: every time her phone rings, she shakes like a leaf, especially when "Mom" shows up on the caller I.D. Candy spends all of her time writing, but she dropped all of her coursework this semester. I have nightmares and can't bear to drive anymore because every pothole feels like—" I crush my napkin in my fists, changing course. "What have we gained, exactly? Because from where I'm sitting, all I see is loss. That pack Angus brought here? Most of them are dead. Leigh, James—"

Angus slams his fist on the tabletop, rattling the glassware. "That's enough." His voice rumbles through my chest wall like a bass line. His jaw is a right angle, the vein in his temple pulsing in time with his heartbeat. It was cruel to mention James. I may as well have kicked Angus in the balls. I rise from the table, tossing my wrinkled napkin onto my empty plate. "I'm going home. I don't feel much like celebrating tonight."

No one follows me, though I can hear Angus apologizing profusely. "I don't know what's gotten into him, Granny. I'm so—" I don't want to hear the rest. As I stride down the driveway, I realize I've forgotten my coat. My house keys are in the pocket, but I don't dare go back inside. The wind whips, tousling my hair and tugging at my clothes like a playground bully. I bow my head to avoid the brunt of it, stuffing my hands into the pockets of my slacks.

I walk along the narrow shoulder, careful to avoid the cattail-laden embankment. If I misstep, I'll tumble into the runnel, soaking my shoes in the freezing brook that threads through the culverts. With my luck, the fall will snap my ankle, exposing a nubbin of bone to the filthy water, the natural habitat of mosquitos and Big Gulps tossed out of car windows. I pass two neighbors' bungalows before Angus catches up to me, my coat in-hand.

If I stop walking, I'm certain that the wind chill will make my muscles as rigid as chicken cutlets forgotten in the freezer. Angus keeps pace with me, draping my coat over my shoulders like a cape. "What the fuck was that, Hunt?"

I thread my arms through the coat's sleeves and zip it up to my chin. "I'm tired of pretending. Aren't you?"

"I don't know what you mean," Angus says. A passing car's headlights throw our shadows out in front of us. His silhouette dwarfs mine in both length and breadth. It's as though the world can't help but remind me of how different we are at every turn.

"I'm tired of pretending that everything is fine!" I'm too loud, and my voice bounces through the culverts. *Fi-yi-yi-ine!* A seagull, roosting atop a concrete drain, shrieks as if to say, *Can you keep it down?* We pass a streetlight, and I catch a glimpse of Angus' face. He's puzzled, his teeth dimpling his bottom lip.

Perhaps he really isn't pretending at all. When we met, he spoke frankly of the barbarism of his people. He abides by laws outside of the humans' purview, written in blood and notarized by teeth. Surely, his savage circumstances rewired his brain, tempering the electrical current that jumps between synapses. He doesn't think like I do because we are not the same species. We are hardly the same genus.

"I don't belong here," I manage around the lump in my throat. "I'm not equipped for this." For a brief moment, I feel unfathomable relief. I've given a name to the fixation that has doggedly nipped at my heels, growing larger with every passing day.

"It's just dinner, Hunter." Angus sighs, clearly exasperated.

Finally, we reach the bungalow we share. My Camry is parked in the driveway, shrouded in a tarp. While the damage to its front end has been repaired, the blood and brain matter buffed out, I can't bear to look at it. I could sell it, but that seems wrong, somehow. I'd left the porch light on when we'd left, and an eclipse of

8

moths orbit the bulb. One flies too close and—*plink!*—its powdery wings crumple. I step up onto the porch step, and for the first time, Angus and I are on equal ground. "No, *no*, you're not *listening*," I say. "Why aren't you listening?"

"Babe," Angus takes my hand, giving my fingers a squeeze. "I'm not trying to be obtuse here, I'm really not. I know you've been feeling depressed. How could you not be? You're on the phone with the insurance company nearly every day. You are working in cramped quarters—here *and* at the café. We hardly get a moment to ourselves."

Angus alludes to problems with concrete solutions. He wants me to focus on what I, a human, can fix. I think of a parent jangling keys in their toddler's face to distract from a red-faced tantrum. *Look here, Hunter!* That's how he thinks of me, isn't it?

"Angus, I killed someone for you—for this pack. But I'm still not a part of your world. Why is that?"

Angus leans against the porch's banister, crossing his arms over his broad chest. I catch a brief glimpse of the "J" tattooed on his ring finger. "You shouldn't be worrying about that," he says.

I laugh, though there's no humor in it. "I know you aren't human, but surely, you understand that humans have feelings, right?" It's a low blow. I may as well have called him a monster.

Angus jerks as though I've slapped him across the face. His lips pull away from his once-squarish teeth, now sharp and numerous. In the jaundiced glow of the porchlight, they appear discolored. A growl rumbles through his chest. "You aren't acting like yourself."

I flip through my keychain to find the house key, distinct from the others because the bow is wrapped in a layer of duct tape, my initials scrawled in sharpie. Over time, the ink has feathered somewhat, leaving only an "H.B" shaped smudge. "That's funny." I chuckle as I slot the key in the lock. "Because you are acting very much like yourself right now."

When Angus rips the porch's handrail off the balusters and throws it into the yard, I don't bother to look back. Loose nails bounce off the porch steps. *Ping, ping, plink!* I shut the door and lean against it, listening to the crunch of gravel as he walks away.

CHAPTER 2
(HENRY)

———◁◆▷———

Sevierville, Tennessee—June 1970

My father is a forest fire. I must always check which way the wind is blowing before getting too close.

I loiter outside of the house long after my mother's truck has pulled away from the curb, pretending to admire a tuft of yellow dandelions growing out of a fissure in the pavement. I can still feel the ghost of her kiss on my cheek, and I know that it will evaporate as soon as I pass through the threshold. Love has no jurisdiction inside the Fairbanks house.

He had to have heard the truck pull up. The engine hacks as though fighting a severe case of croup. If I keep him waiting for too long, he'll be apoplectic. I can hear him now: *what are you hiding, Henry Lee?* I fish my house key from my overnight tote and slot it into the lock. I am relieved, albeit perplexed, to find the living room empty. Usually, when I come home, he's waiting for me on the sofa like a guard dog at the end of its chain, hackles raised.

Despite the summer's heat, the air conditioning unit is off; the room is stagnant and still. The spider plant on the mantle droops in its painted pot, the narrow leaves brown and brittle at the edges. The heavy curtains are partially drawn, letting only a narrow shaft of light play across the rust-orange carpet. I take off my shoes and socks before stepping onto it because I like the feeling of the squashy, shaggy fibers between my toes. This afternoon, though, I find no solace in it; something is wrong. I can sense it, just like our cat, Cindy, could sense that she was dying. Even before the tumor caused her back legs to drag and her bowels to release on the kitchen linoleum, she knew.

"Dad?" I call. My voice sounds flat in the airless room. I drop my tote beside my shoes and head down the hall. Perhaps he's in his study. I pass my own room, the door ajar, and peek in. It's just as I left it last weekend: the bed unmade, the Mickey Mouse bedspread in a heap on the floor; G.I. Joe action figures marching across my desk; and a dresser with unclean laundry piled on top. I can see the stains on the knees of my baseball knickers from my slide into home plate. I wince at the sight, remembering the thump of the catcher's mitt on my shoulder. *Y'er out, Fairbanks!*

The door to the study is closed. When I press my ear to it, I can hear shuffling inside—a dry cough muffled by a fist. "Dad?" I call again, cracking the door.

He's never in his study during the day, preferring to laze on the couch in the company of Mr. Art Linkletter. The study is for his nighttime toiling: listening to AM radio and downing Rheingolds. The intermittent crush of the cans and *pssst* of the tab provides the soundtrack for my dreams.

I keep my hand on the knob. If he's feeling inhospitable, I'll have to close the door quickly to avoid being hit in the head by a thrown Rolodex or paperweight. Part of me hopes he'll do it. I don't like his study, the walls adorned with grotesque hunting trophies. I find their glass eyes particularly unsettling. They seem to track me around the room. He is most proud of the moose head mounted behind his desk. When he sits just so, it makes him look as if he has grown enormous palmate antlers.

"I'm home," I add, just in case he's forgotten where I've been. He often forgets about me altogether. Sometimes, if I walk into the living room after being in my room for too long, he jumps as though he's seen a ghost.

"Come in," he croaks. He sounds like the fat Spadefoot frog I once found squatting in a puddle beneath the rain spout: sluggish, dyspeptic, and hoarse. He's clearly been chain-smoking, even though he promised my mother he'd quit.

Hazy, bluish smoke hangs in the air. making my eyes water. Even hours after I leave, I can still smell the sulfurous odor permeating my clothes. When I was younger, I thought there was a frightened skunk trapped inside the wall. I would press my ear against the knotty pine paneling, convinced I would be able to hear the animal's scratching. When I couldn't hear it, I imagined it had been mummified, sandwiched between the sheets of drywall like a slice of bologna. Now that I'm thirteen years old, I know better.

Milton Fairbanks is a man who has been told his entire life that he's too tall. His body is riddled with a lifetime of apologies: kyphosis of the spine, hunched shoulders, and knee joints that crackle like Rice Krispies. Conversely, I'm small, like my mother. Even sitting behind his desk, he is as intimidating and as fearsome as a giant. I often have nightmares wherein he grows taller than the house and swallows me whole.

"How's your mother?" he asks without looking at me. He jabs his joint into his ashtray, splitting the paper. The pungent odor of spent stems fills my nose.

I am too frightened to venture inside. I keep my hand on the doorknob, turning it this way and that. My palms are slick with sweat. "She says 'hello,'" I reply, licking at my dry lips.

Finally, my father deigns to look at me. He presses his lips together as if trying to stop a deluge of vomit from escaping. "Come in here, boy. Sit down."

When I step into the smoky room, I realize we aren't alone. A man wearing a funny dress and skullcap occupies the leather armchair in the adjacent corner, his hands steepled beneath his fleshy chin. He doesn't look at me, his heavily lidded eyes trained on the carpet. Another identically dressed man stands behind the seated one, his hands resting on the chair back. With his long, stubbly neck, bald head, and broad shoulders, he reminds me of the vulture in *Snow White and the Seven Dwarves*. A skullcap rests upon his bare scalp, seemingly held in place by religious conviction alone.

When he looks at me, his smile is so wide that I swear I can see all thirty-two of his yellowy, chiclet-shaped teeth. His dimples are trenches cut into the weathered rock of his cheeks and his lower lip shakes as if maintaining a smile requires the utmost physical exertion. I half-expect a bead of sweat to trickle down his lined brow. His eyes are a brilliant blue, albeit joyless. It's as though he's wearing two faces: the grin of a circus clown and the thousand-yard stare of a shellshocked soldier.

"Sit down, Henry Lee," my father repeats, gesturing to the folding chair in the center of the room. I recognize it; it's one of the chairs we pull out of the garage on Thanksgiving. There's a brown, crusty stain on the seat. I think it might be gravy. I hope it's gravy. Gingerly, I sit on the very edge, tipping the back legs up off the carpet. Behind me, one of the men sniffles.

"How's Samuel?" My father spits out the name as if the syllables taste caustic upon his tongue. On the desktop, his hands clench into fists, the knuckles blanching. The question surprises me. He rarely asks about my stepfather. He certainly never calls him by name. Instead, Samuel is referred to as simply *him*.

"Fine," I murmur, tugging at a loose string on the knee of my Levi's. I can hear my mother's admonishment in my head. *Don't pull on it, Henry. You'll unravel them!*

"Just 'fine'?"

I don't answer, turning in my chair to look at the two men. The Vulture is still smiling at me. I have to resist the urge to hook my fingers in my lips and pull them wide. *This is what you look like*, I want to say. My father snaps his fingers to regain my attention.

"Who are they?" I ask.

"Don't worry about them. There was a full moon last night. Did you know that?"

I shake my head. I'm not sure how my father knows that. Milton Fairbanks is a man whose feet are firmly planted on the Earth, his eyes never straying above the horizon line. While he bought me a telescope for my birthday last month, he never looked through it—not once. When I came home from school to excitedly tell him about Belka and Strelka, the first dogs to successfully travel into orbit and survive reentry aboard the Russian spacecraft *Vostok*, he merely huffed and said: "It should have been some American dog named Lady or Max."

"What did he do last night?"

"Who?" I furtively glance at the men again. The Vulture waggles his fingers at me.

My father slams his palm against the desktop. I jump. "Pay attention, Henry Lee. *Samuel*. What did *Samuel* do?"

My heart clatters against my chest wall. "We watched television while mama made lasagna. *The Flintstones* was on. It was the episode where Fred forgets Dino's birthday, and—" Mid-sentence, I pause. My father's face is as red as the cherry-flavored dome of a bomb pop. He's sweating profusely, perspiration dampening the collar of his button-down. He doesn't want to hear about *The Flintstones*. "We ate at the table. Mama doesn't like when we watch television during meals, you know. Then we went out to check on Barley Mae."

"Barley Mae?" The Vulture's voice is like ice cold water poured down the back of my shirt. It's strangely breathy, as though his clerical collar is too tight. I don't turn to look at him, convinced that I'll see a serpent's forked tongue slither out of his lipless mouth.

"One of the ewes on the farm. She was pregnant, and Samuel thought she would give birth any minute, so we'd gone out every hour or so to check on her. When we went out after dinner, one of the lamb's legs was sticking out of her. Barley was trying to squeeze it out—bleating, pacing, and carrying on—but she couldn't do it. Samuel said we had to help her, so he grabbed the lamb's leg and pulled. I thought for sure the leg was just going to pop off with how hard he was pulling. Eventually, the lamb came out, along with a whole bunch of blood and mess, but—"

I'd been trying very hard not to think about the lamb all day. Every time I thought I'd stuffed the memory deep enough, it would pop up at the most inopportune times: trying to remember how to spell s-o-l-i-l-o-q-u-y; taking my turn at four square; or while sucking Jell-O through my teeth at lunchtime. The lamb was small, long-limbed, and slick with amniotic fluid. At first, I thought its fur was made flat by the squeeze through the birth canal, but when I touched it, it lacked the telltale whorls and curls. The lamb was hairless. Its little pink tongue stuck out as if tasting the air. It could do little else. Its skull was grotesquely misshapen, its ears were nubs, its nose was probiscal, and it only had one watery eye, smack dab in the middle of its head. I was struck by how long its eyelashes were, even gummed together with pus.

"It only had one eye," I finally blurt out. "It died within a half-hour." I don't tell the men that I cried when its wheezing stopped.

"Cyclopia," the Vulture says, with a self-satisfied hum. "Milton, animals are sensitive to demonic forces. Especially livestock that witnessed the birth of Christ. There are many cases of animals who've experienced fear birthing defective offspring." I want to tell the man that Barley Mae is only three years old and that she certainly wasn't lying in the straw next to the Christ child's manger, watching him receive gifts of frankincense and myrrh. But I'm a little afraid I'll cry if I talk about the ewe and how she bawled for her baby long after Samuel gently wrapped it up and took it away.

"After the lamb died, what did Samuel do?" my father asks. He isn't looking at me. Instead, he looks over my shoulder at the Vulture. It's as though they are having a conversation I am not privy to.

"He sent me inside because it was a school night and I needed to take a bath. When he came to say good night, he smelled like woodsmoke. He said he burned the lamb's body."

The older clergyman rises from his seat with a sigh. He shuffles over as if the soles of his shoes are leaden. He rests his heavy hands on my shoulders, and my nostrils fill with the sickly-sweet odor of flop sweat and Werther's Originals. I peer up at him, but all I can see from this angle are his bristly chins and cavernous nostrils. When he speaks, they flare. "A Black

Mass," he breathes. "A sacrificial lamb, a pyre, the boy is surely next!"

Milton lurches out of his chair, nearly toppling it. "My friends and I need to talk. Go to bed, Henry Lee."

I don't tell him it's only four o'clock in the afternoon. When the man takes his hands off of my shoulders, I dart out of the stifling room. The cool hallway is a relief, and my room is a refuge. The men's voices rumble on the other side of the wall, but they are indistinct. It's akin to listening to a mosquito buzz around a window, knowing it will leave me be; finding an exit is paramount, whereas alighting on my arm may result in a hearty *smack*!

I linger in my room until the sun goes down, expecting my father to come get me for dinner, but he never comes. He doesn't appear when I go into the kitchen to make a sandwich nor when I tuck myself into bed. When I sleep, I dream of sheep going to slaughter.

"Wake up, son."

It's pitch-dark in my room, save for the greenish glow of my nightlight. The meager light source is meant to be a comfort, but it only serves to lengthen the shadows on the wall. When I am alone, they seem particularly chimeric—shifting into a leviathan with myriad teeth or a waifish ghoul with impossibly long fingers. Tonight, the shadow is in the shape of my father. This form is not a comfort either.

I sit up in bed. Backlit by the nightlight, my father's features are amorphous, indistinct. Perhaps the man kneeling beside my bed isn't my father at all. A nightmare, realized. Gooseflesh prickles on my bare arms.

19

"Daddy?" I whisper. I want to reach out and touch him, but I'm worried he won't be corporeal. What would it feel like to touch a shadow? Will my skin crawl, as if I've plunged my arm into an anthill? Or will it be like the time Eddie McNair dared me to jump into Red Lynx reservoir on the coldest day in February? I thought that I would never stop shivering.

"It was a full moon last night, Henry," my father whispers. "Did you know that?"

"You told me," I mumble, rubbing at my sleep-crusted eyes. I can smell beer on his breath, oozing out of his pores.

"Tie his hands." A figure loiters by the door, the nightlight reflecting off of his bald head. "Once we start, he can't slip away." The voice is a sigh—a death rattle. "It's important we finish the rite, so we can save his soul."

"Daddy?" I repeat his name like a wish. "Who's that?" I push off my Mickey Mouse comforter and throw my legs over the side of the bed, but there's nowhere to go. My father is in the way.

"Listen to me, Henry Lee," my father murmurs. "It is important that you listen to everything we say." Tenderly, he takes my hand and wraps a bungee cord around my thin wrist. At first, he is gentle, but when I try to yank my hand away, his grip tightens. He lashes my wrists, causing my pisiform bones to grind together in a particularly unpleasant way. When I start to cry, he avoids my eyes.

"Daddy!" I blubber, tears trickling down my cheeks. "What's happening?" I wrack my brain over the last few hours, searching for any impropriety I may have committed. Had I left the peanut butter out after making my sandwich? No, no I didn't think so.

The shadowy figure flips the light switch, filling my bedroom with light. My father secures my arms to the headboard. I kick my feet, my pistoning heels rattling the box spring. *Thwunk, thwunk, thwunk!* "The feet too, Milton," the man—the Vulture—says softly. "We can't give the demon any leeway."

The demon?

It's as though I've become invisible. Neither man reacts to my wailing. My father ties my ankles much as he did my wrists, trussing them to the footboard. I feel as though I've been stretched beyond what my body is capable of; a tearing sensation blooms in my armpits and extends down my ribs with every trembling exhale.

"Hello again, Henry," the Vulture says. "I'm Father Ricci. You've been cavorting with the enemy, you poor lost lamb. We have to make sure you are clean."

I don't understand him. Perhaps I'm not catching every word. I can hardly hear anything beyond the pounding of my heartbeat. I am certain that my heart is midway up my esophagus now and that I will unceremoniously vomit the slippery knot of muscle onto my bedspread. I am too frightened to remain whole. I want to break apart, to become dust.

The Vulture—Father Ricci—draws a cross above my prone body with two fingers, then pulls what looks like a squat, metal wand out of his pocket. When he flicks it, droplets of cool water sprinkle upon my cheeks, mixing with my tears and snot. "Our Father, who art in Heaven, hallowed be thy name," he murmurs.

"I—I don't understand," I wail, flopping on the mattress like a dying salmon. "Daddy!"

"I'm here, son." A hand—his hand—rests upon my shoulder. I know the terrain of those hands just as well as I know the route to Ridgerton Elementary. His uncharacteristic gentleness is the most terrifying thing of all.

Father Ricci continues to pray, the words familiar but ultimately meaningless. I attend Sunday School every week, but I spend the sessions goofing off, unraveling God's Eyes to play Cat's Cradle. "I know that Samuel Campbell has gotten his claws into you," my father continues, "but he can't have you. No demon will take my son."

Father Ricci places his fingers on my forehead. "I command you, unclean spirit, by the mysteries of the incarnation, passion, resurrection, and ascension of our Lord Jesus Christ, by the descent of the Holy Spirit, by the coming of our Lord for judgment, that you tell me your name!"

"Please," I cry, tugging against the restraints. "Please, I'm just Henry. Daddy, don't you believe me?"

Knoxville, Tennessee—Present Day

A siren's shriek wakes me, red lights strafing across my rain-streaked window. I left the rental car idling, and smooth jazz trills through the speakers. I didn't intend to doze, but the warmth emanating from the heater and the rumble of the engine lulled me into something resembling sleep. It was fitful at best; without a double dose of Ambien to quiet my mind, I was plagued by nightmares. The dreams are a symptom of the disease that is disquietude.

The digital clock reads 11:15 a.m. Visiting hours at the hospital started over an hour and a half ago. *Shit!* Turning off the engine, I take a quick swig of cold gas station coffee to wet my uncomfortably dry mouth. *Was I snoring?* I flip down the visor to examine my reflection. My ash-colored hair is unkempt, the roots oily. I scrape my fingers through it, pushing it off my forehead. The grease makes it stay in place, save for the cowlick at my hairline. The slouchy bags under my red-rimmed eyes give me a particularly hang-dog look, but there's no fixing that.

"I'm Detective Dupin," I practice in the mirror, using the alias I stole from Edgar Allen Poe's mysteries. "I'm here to get a statement." My reflection scowls back at me. "No, *no*. How about: 'I just want to—no, *need* to—ask you a few questions'?" My stomach roils. If I don't go now, I'll lose my nerve. I slap the visor shut.

I hurry to the hospital's entrance, ducking my head to avoid the freezing rain. A fat droplet dribbles beneath the collar of my jacket and moistens my shirt. Under the portico, an ambulance idles, its back doors left wide open. The gurney is gone, the floor littered with bits of soiled gauze and a spent salbutamol cartridge.

The atrium of Knoxville General is the crown jewel in its new 250 million dollar tiara. It resembles a mausoleum or, rather, an Apple Store: stark and sterile. Everything is glass and stainless steel. A living wall—covered in flowering sedum and geometric succulents—flanks reception. I pause just inside the entryway, wondering if I've somehow walked into the wrong building. It didn't look like this when I was a kid, but that was over fifty years ago now, wasn't it? My chest tightens, and I rub at my sternum with my knuckles. I read somewhere that pain is supposed to be grounding.

"I'm here to see a patient," I say to the receptionist when it's my turn. "Tara Johnson. I'm her uncle Sutton Johnson."

I am surprised when the receptionist hands me a laminated visitor's badge, points me in the direction of the Medical/Surgical Floor and gives me the room number. She barely gives me a second glance. I had spent hours scrolling through Tara's Instagram feed, clicking on the people she tagged in photos, trying to find the perfect alias. Sutton fit the bill well enough: mid-sixties, with a penchant for sleeveless tees bought exclusively from Tractor Supply. According to his bio, he bleeds red, white, and fuckin' blue! Yee-haw.

I take the elevator to the third floor. Unlike the lobby, Med-Surg is anachronistic. The elevator may as well have been a time machine. The cinderblock walls are painted with a thick coat of beige. Drips and chips mottle the already craggy surface. Beneath the beige is a layer of institutional green. It gives the walls a sickly quality, like the skin of a patient looking for an emesis basin. When I was a kid, all of the hospitals were that bilious, diluted pea soup color. It was meant to soothe the doctors, who spent their days cutting up and stitching together red, raw man-meat. Red and green are complementary—like Christmas.

Tara is in room 327, which is, thankfully, several doors down from the nurse's station. I can't afford to have anyone overhear. A bored-looking nurse in burgundy scrubs glances at me but returns her attention to her phone. I stuff the visitor badge into the back pocket of my jeans.

As I push the door open, I rap my knuckles against it. A cop wouldn't wait for an invitation. I try very hard to stand up straight. I have a bad habit of slouching. If I could walk with my knuckles dragging on the linoleum like a gorilla, I would. "Miss Johnson? I'm Detective Dupin. Can I have a moment of your time?"

I wince. *Come on, Henry. You sound like a seedy car salesman!*

The room has two beds, but only one is occupied. Tara is a rail-thin girl, with skin so pale that it is nearly translucent; though, I expect that's due to the blood loss. She's wearing a hospital gown, and the tie at the nape of her neck has come loose, revealing the cap of her shoulder and a tattoo of a koi fish. She presses the button on the rail to raise the head of the bed until she's sitting up. It's clearly a struggle. Her petal-pink lips blanch to a corpse-like pallor. "I've already talked to the police."

"Now you're speaking to me," I say, pulling a chair up to her bedside. The legs squeal against the linoleum. "It's procedure," I add as an afterthought. Isn't that what they always say on *Law & Order*?

Tara pulls the thin, woven blanket up around her midsection. Her hands tremble just slightly, and I remind myself to be gentle. She's experienced something horrifying. That was apparent even over the police scanner. *10-91 at 182 Falcone Boulevard. Patient is unresponsive and bleedin' out. Call Animal Control and tell 'em to bring the tranq guns. I repeat: we have a 10-91, and it must have been a big fuckin' animal!*

"It will only take a few minutes," I assure her. "Just tell me what happened that night, and I'll be out of your hair."

Tara picks at the hem of the blanket, worrying the string through her fingers like a rosary. I have to look away. "I was at work, and I met a girl. We went to Culvers to drink and dance, then went back to my apartment. We were kissing and—" She releases a shaky breath. "I—I don't know how to say it without sounding crazy."

"Tara, when you've been on the force for as long as I have, you see some truly crazy things. I promise you, you're not even going to get on the top ten list." She doesn't laugh at my joke. Instead, she turns her face away, looking toward the empty bed and, beyond it, the window. The sun is nearing its highest point in the sky, but it can't penetrate the drab swath of cumulonimbus clouds. If I didn't know any better, I would assume it's near dusk.

"We needed the rain," Tara mumbles. "At least, that's what my mom always said whenever it stormed—drought or not. She's a glass-half-full type. I'm trying really hard to be optimistic now but—" She gingerly rests her hand on her right leg or, rather, the swath of blankets under which her right leg should have been.

"Tell me what happened," I repeat gently. "At least then, I can get you justice. I know it's not the same as having your leg back, but it's something."

With the blanket clenched in her fist, Tara begins again. She speaks through gritted teeth, and I have to lean forward to hear her. "We were kissing, and she knelt down to undress me. She was wearing a beanie, and I took it off because it was the only part of her I could reach. I don't know if she put something in my drink or I drank more than I thought, but her ears ... there was something wrong with her ears."

"Her ears?" A lightning bolt of excitement courses through me. My intuition was right.

"Yeah." Reliving the events of the night before brings color to Tara's cheeks. Or, is it a fever? Her nostrils flare, her breathing fast as though we are on a jog together. "They were pointy, like an elf in *The Lord of the Rings*, except they were covered in silky, silver fur. Before I could ask about it, she bit me."

"So, what you're saying is: a 'girl' mauled you so badly that you had to have your leg amputated?" I try to sound incredulous though, inwardly, I'm electrified. This is exactly what I was hoping to hear.

"You don't believe me."

Perhaps I sounded too skeptical. "Like I said: this isn't even in the top ten. You mentioned her ears. Was anything else ... unusual about her?"

Tara chews at her bottom lip, her brow furrowing. "I don't remember much beyond that. Everything gets out-of-focus after that. But, her teeth—her teeth were so sharp. Sometimes, at my work, I help with prep in the kitchen, chopping vegetables, mostly. I once cut myself with a paring knife. I bled like a stuck pig for hours afterward. This? This was like getting stabbed with a hundred of them, all at once, over and over."

I can hear voices in the hall. Perhaps it's best I go now, before someone more lucid comes in and asks for Detective Dupin's credentials. I bolt upward out of my chair. "One more question before I leave you to rest," I manage through trembling lips. *Calm down, Henry. You're going to blow it!* "What was the girl's name?"

Tara grimaces. "Haley. I don't know her last name."

I think that I might.

CHAPTER 3
(ANGUS)

⊲◆⊳

Despite the chill, I work with the windows open. It's how Ama prefers it. "If I can't smell the ocean, I may as well be dead," she says when I protest. "If I get a sniffle, so be it. I'm made of much tougher stuff than you think!" She wrinkles her nose when I cover her lap in a knitted blanket, but she doesn't toss it aside.

The Christmas tree box has been taped and re-taped. The edges are soft and battered; it's not quite a rectangle anymore. I carefully pick at the tape, but when I peel it away, a layer of cardboard comes with it. The artificial tree inside smells musty—far from the sharp and woody smell of pine. I'm secretly glad for it. Pine makes me think of Oregon, and Oregon makes me think of loss.

A breeze trickles through the half-drawn curtains, ruffling my hair. It smells like brine. *If I can't smell the ocean, I may as well be dead*. The ocean reminds me of Hunter, and without him, I would be dead too. The endeavor took my eye, but it took something far more invaluable from him: his serenity. It had been excised from him like a teratoma, leaving a crater in his gut. I've been trying to fill it ever since, to no avail.

Hunter has been in the shower for thirty minutes. I keep looking at my watch, watching the minute hand creep around the sterling silver face. Hunter gifted it to me on the anniversary of our first kiss. Surely, he won't fault me for keeping time now.

Loitering outside, I listen to the running water. "Hunter?" I call, rapping my knuckles against the door. He doesn't answer. A greasy, unsettled feeling roils around in my stomach. Since the café was destroyed, he's been as bristly as a porcupine. He turns away when I try to kiss him. He ducks under my arm when I embrace him, except just before excusing himself to the bathroom, he leaned over and kissed me, unprompted.

I throw open the door. Humidity slaps my cheeks as if trying to rouse me from a dream. Both the mirrors and shower cubicle are hazy, condensation puddling on the countertop. I have to shuffle to keep from slipping on the slick floor. The sandblasted glass of the shower cubicle makes its occupant look like an abstract portrait—a smear of flesh tones.

I wrench open the shower door, and I find Hunter sitting on the floor, his knees drawn up to his chest. His sudsy hair lays wetly upon his forehead. It appears as though he simply sat down mid-wash, unable to muster the energy to continue. When he looks up at me, I can see the weariness etched upon his face. I don't know how I missed it before.

I am so relieved to find him safe that I join him inside the narrow cubicle, throwing my arms around his hunched shoulders. His body stiffens. "You'll ruin your clothes," he mumbles into the soaked lapel of my shirt.

"You scared me," I gasp, my voice wobbling with fettered emotion. My sneakers fill up with water, soaking my socks. "Why didn't you answer me?"

"I didn't hear you." Hunter wriggles out of my embrace, scrambling to his feet. His movements are coltish. "My foot is asleep," he complains as he shifts from foot to foot, slapping the soles against the floor. He throws his head back beneath the stream, scrubbing at his scalp.

I rise too, leaning back against the cool, tiled wall. His body blocks most of the water from the shower head, but errant droplets tickle my arms. "Hunter," I murmur, "please talk to me."

He turns slightly away from me, wetting his face. Eyes screwed up tight, he reaches blindly for the pink bottle of face wash but only succeeds in knocking it off of the shelf. I bend to retrieve it and squirt a dollop into his outstretched palm. With a grunt of gratitude, he lathers his face and the scraggly beard he's cultivated over the last few weeks. It doesn't quite suit him, but there's a certain boyish charm to it. "Are you just not going to talk to me?" I ask.

Suds trickle down his neck as he rinses his face clean. Finally, he opens his eyes. They are as brown as the bark of a Sassafras tree and, like its root, are more than capable of masking even the most undesirable tang. For a moment, I don't remember why my

31

nerves are twanging, why I can't quite seem to catch my breath. "I have a lot on my mind," Hunter says coolly. "I can't just brush it aside—call it 'pack business.' I'm not like you."

He turns the water off and cracks open the glass door to reach for the towel draped upon the rack. Despite the steam hanging in the air, a chill rushes into the cubicle. My nipples harden painfully beneath the clinging fabric of my sodden shirt. "What do you mean?" I can't help but sound testy. His words sound accusatory.

Hunter dries himself while standing on the bath mat. He swipes the towel under his arms, down the smooth plane of his stomach, and between his legs. Then, he wraps it tightly around his waist. "I'm not trying to start a fight, Angus. You told me yourself: 'sometimes, you have to make a hard decision for the greater good.' I can't seem to get there. I know what I did was the same thing, but—"

Hunter swipes away the condensation on the mirror, leaning so close that his nose touches the glass. He squeezes at an invisible zit on his cheek. "But," he continues, "I can't make the mental leap to the place where I feel anything close to equanimity. I just feel like a murderer."

Stepping out of the shower stall, my feet dwarf the wet footprints he left on the mat. My clothes drip. "You aren't—"

A sharp look silences me. He doesn't want platitudes. "We aren't the same, Angus. After what happened, that's becoming all the more apparent. I'm not made of the right stuff to be in your world. I'm …

breaking." A sob bubbles to the surface, contorting his features. I am suddenly cognizant of how the last year has changed him. He's aged a decade, worry lines creasing his forehead and dark circles rimming his eyes.

"I thought you said this wasn't a fight," I say testily. I feel as though we are standing very close to a cliff edge, and he's liable to throw himself off. Or, perhaps, he intends to push me.

Hunter rests his palms on the porcelain countertop, hanging his head. "I'm done fighting," he whispers. "I've been trying—lord knows I've tried. Can't you see that?"

He won't look at me. Why won't he look at me?

I lurch forward, grabbing for his elbow. "Just spit it out," I plead. "Just say it."

Hunter flinches away from my touch. He may as well have punched me in the jaw. "I can't do this anymore."

"I hope you like marshmallows," Toby says as she slowly waddles in from the kitchen, carrying three steaming mugs of hot cocoa. She holds them at arm's length as if afraid of getting burned, two in her right hand and the third in her left. Jumbo-sized marshmallows bob above the rim like icebergs in the North Atlantic.

The living room, laden with antiques, is perilous on any given day, but the Christmas boxes are additional hindrances. She edges around a Rubbermaid full of ornaments, cursing under her breath as cocoa sloshes down the side of one of the mugs and soaks her knuckles. I pop up from the floor to help her, taking two of the mugs from her hands. "You should have asked for help," I scold the young woman.

"I'm pregnant, not dead," Toby reminds me coolly. "But thank you, *Aggie*."

As I hand one of the mugs to Ama, I catch my grandmother smiling. "It's been lonely in Wharton for so long," she explains. "For years, I haven't bothered putting up the tree because it's just been me. But this year, I have a pack."

"And Alexandre," Toby reminds her with a wink.

"And Alexandre," Ama relents. The infatuated Frenchman has doggedly pursued my grandmother for months, though she's thwarted every very public proposal. Once, he sashayed into Ebb and Flow with a string quartet playing *La Vie en Rose*, and she dumped an iced latte on his head. It's become a sort of game for them: a ruse to dissimulate a very real relationship. At sundown, I often find them sitting side-by-side on the back deck listening to old Frank Sinatra records. They never touch, but there's a palpable intimacy there. If there wasn't, Ama would simply eat him and use his metacarpals to pick her teeth clean afterward.

Wordlessly, I place my cup of cocoa on the coffee table and turn back to my task. I wish I could share her exuberance. I jam the bottom bough into the tree stand, screwing in the eye bolts to secure it. I stack two more boughs before I realize Toby is talking to me. She waves a hand in front of my face, her stacked brace-lets jangling. One of them is made up of squarish letter beads, spelling out C-A-M-D-E-N, the town where she grew up. "You should never forget where you came from," she told me once, "even if people think it's nowhere special—it made you, didn't it?"

"Is Hunter coming?" she repeats.

I sigh, standing on tiptoes to place the crown of the tree in its slot. "I don't know."

"You can't be mad at each other forever," she groans. "Can't you just kiss and make up? It's almost Christmas."

"You 'can't do this anymore'? What the fuck does that mean?" I snarl, following Hunter into our bedroom. I scrape off my water-laden shirt, dropping it onto the carpet.

Hunter doesn't answer as he pulls a pair of boxer briefs and a tie-dyed Ebb and Flow tee from the squat dresser. The shirt musses his still-damp hair, making it stick straight up. I don't like the version of Hunter that emerged from the shower cubicle chrysalis: preternaturally calm and collected, nary a hint of anxiety in his movements.

Hunter is, by nature, an anxious person. His hands perpetually shake except when he pours crema into coffee to create intricate designs. He wears his emotions on his sleeve, unabashedly weeping during romance films or when he's feeling particularly frustrated. This Hunter is behaving like an automaton, every response pre-programmed by an algorithm.

"It means that something has to change," he finally says as he tugs a pair of gray-wash jeans up over his butt. "I think I've finally figured out what it is. It came to me after Ama's birthday party. I want to be a wolf."

His words are so preposterous that I laugh. I slap my hands against my knees, unable to contain the guffaw that bursts forth. No one of sound mind would ask for this. It's an affliction, brought on by faulty genetics or an infection, awakening something vestigial in the forebrain and folding proteins. It lights up every available pain receptor, cracking the body in half like a wishbone on Thanksgiving. It is a prion that doesn't have the decency to kill its host.

My response clearly isn't what Hunter expected; he frowns. "Angus, if I'm in the pack—really in the pack—I can get past what happened. We can be together in the way you deserve. You wouldn't have to be gentle with me when—"

"You don't realize what you're asking of me, not really. You don't need to wear fur to be in this pack or to be with me," I interrupt, resting my hands on his shoulders. I forget to be tender, and he winces, raising both eyebrows as if to say, See?

He shrugs off my touch. "Please, Angus," he wheedles, sounding very much like a child begging for the new toy in the shop window. "I need this. You have to see that we're standing on uneven footing. When there's danger, I'm always waiting outside or hiding behind you. Even at Ama's birthday dinner last month, you got to sit at the table, and I was relegated to the deck with the other humans. I may as well be on a leash."

Where he sees a power imbalance, I see a reminder of my own humanity. He is not a pet nor something fragile that I hold in my hands to test my own mettle. "You don't 'need' this. This will kill you. You think it'll make you strong, but really, it weaponizes your weaknesses." I throw up my hands. "Besides, I couldn't make you wolfish even if I wanted to."

"Haley can," Hunter retorts. "It takes the bite of a rabid wolf, you told me that yourself. Haley was rabid. She said she would help me."

"You've spoken to Haley about this?" Anger ratchets up my jaw, my teeth scraping together so hard that they squeal. Paresthesia prickles on the back of my hands, semi-translucent fur bursting from my pores. I clench my fists, keenly aware of my nails growing sharp. They dig into my palms. I imagine the young woman lazing on our couch in the living room, her sock-clad feet propped up on the coffee table alongside a sweating can of Fanta. I should drag her out by her hair and dump her in a sand dune. "Is she home? I'd like to tell her she's overstayed her welcome in our fucking house."

"Haley and Candy went to the store," Hunter reminds me. "Angus, please listen to me. If you don't help me, I'm not sure I can be with you anymore."

"That sounds an awful lot like an ultimatum."

"That's because it is one."

CHAPTER 4
(HUNTER)

————◁◆▷————

T his time of year, the sky is perpetually gray, laden with low-hanging clouds. The air is crisp and damp, so much so that I find myself looking skyward, expecting snowfall. But snow is a rarity on the coast. So much for a white Christmas. Usually, I look at the clouds with a sort of eager, guileless anticipation. *Maybe this year!* I dream of sledding, building snowmen, and languishing in front of a fireplace.

I forgot my scarf. I can picture it slung across the back of the couch, the tricot knit resembling a snake's oblong scales. Angus is always badgering me to hang it on the coat rack in the foyer, but without his exasperated sigh to remind me, I've forgotten again. Gooseflesh prickles on the nape of my neck. I tug my beanie down toward the upturned lapel of my Carhartt coat, but it rides up as soon as I release it.

Still, I linger on the pier, looking out at the horizon line where the surf meets the firmament. With the haze, it is difficult to discern one swath of gray from the other. It's as though Wharton exists inside of a snow globe that's been thoroughly shaken up. If I reach out, I am convinced that I may be able to touch the transparent curve of the dome.

It's strangely comforting. On a clear day, the Atlantic Ocean seems endless, and I imagine how far out I can swim before my body gives out. It's the call of the void, I think. After all, when you tango with death and get lucky enough to walk off the dance floor afterward as we did, you feel more than a little impetuous.

Despite the early morning hour, the red and green twinkle lights adorning the pier's rough-hewn railing are on. Their meager light dances across the seafoam. I picture an anglerfish's bioluminescent lure, or the bright spot on an MRI denoting pain. A slow-rolling calliope rendition of "It's Beginning to Look a Lot Like Christmas" jangles through the speakers on the merry-go-round. The horses—decorated with wreaths and oversized velvet bows—are still, casting grotesque shadows upon the ground. I try not to look at them. Despite the weeks that have passed since, I still have nightmares about the crash.

For a moment after the collision, I am certain that I must have died. A high-pitched ringing fills my ears. I swirl my finger in my ear, trying to make it stop but to no avail. Sodium azide from the deployed airbag drifts around the car's interior, and in my delirium, I want to tilt my head back and catch the flakes on my tongue. Finally, snow!

The car's high beams are on, illuminating the decimated interior of my café. It's as though a bomb went off, leaving behind a postmodern pastiche of splintered

*chair legs, shards of glass, pulverized drywall, and
exposed loops of electrical wiring. Oh, God. A dog
pops its dust-mottled head up from behind an overturned table. No, not a dog—it's much too big to be a
dog. Perhaps it's a Grim, a calamitous portent.*

*The ringing in my head is making it hard to think.
How did I get here? Perhaps there was a tornado, and
I was flung into the building like Dorothy into Oz. No,
that doesn't seem right. Think, Hunter! The wolf—I
remember now—rises, and I see that she's cradling a
limp woman in her arms. Even with her slack face covered in grime and blood, I recognize her. I've known
her since she was just a heartbeat and a smudge on
an ultrasound ("See that, Hunter? That's your sister").
I remember pressing my cheek against the bib of our
mother's overalls, singing so that, when she was born,
we wouldn't have to bother with introductions. When I
clambered up onto the hospital gurney to examine the
red-faced newborn, I was disappointed that she didn't
greet me by name.*

*I drove into the building to rescue my sister. And
Angus. It all comes back to me like a slap: the text message, the plan, Angus' bulging eyes as his larynx was
crushed. I look around wildly. Where's Angus? Maybe
I was too late. Did I hesitate before I slammed my foot
on the accelerator?*

*I feel claustrophobic. I can't breathe. With shaking
hands, I release myself from my seatbelt, throwing my
whole body against the door handle. I can't breathe, I
can't—I need to get out. The door opens, but not very
far. A beam, fallen from the rafters, stands in the way.*

I squeeze out the meager gap, feeling very much like the last bit of toothpaste in the tube.

"Angus?" I call. I'm dizzy—dark shadows usurp the edges of my vision, and I can't seem to blink them away. I grab onto the car door, trying to gulp fresh air, but all I inhale is dust. I imagine it filling my lungs like an hourglass. Time's up.

A pile of debris shifts, and Angus emerges. He's still wolfish, his white fur dingy. When he looks at me, I want to cry. His right eye is ruined, only a mess of blood and vitreous gel left inside the dark, bruised socket. His left eye is undefiled—as blue as ever. "I told you to wait in the car," he grumbles.

"I did." I pick my way around the wreckage, desperately wanting to be close to him. I want to bury my face in his fur, inhale his musk. Perhaps then I won't feel so unmoored, so off-balance. But when I step around the Camry's ruined front end, I am certain that even the warmest embrace will be futile. There will be no repairing me.

Leigh Volkov is wedged beneath the crumpled bumper, her blood smeared on the headlight. I am certain she had been wolfish just before I stood on the accelerator, but now, she is human. Her lithe, dancer's body is bent into a series of acute angles. Her scapula is dislocated, the glenohumeral joint punching through her tissue paper skin. Her semi-attached arm is draped around her neck like a grotesque boa, her broken fingers resting on the opposite shoulder. Her chin rests heavily on a piece of rebar, broken teeth littering the floor like seer stones. I can see my future clearly, and it is bleak.

It's not quite 8 o'clock, but Main Street is already bustling. In Wharton, the winter months are lean times. Just one extra sale might keep the lights on and rent paid until the tourists return come summertime. The sidewalks are well-lit, crisscrossed with garlands, baubles, and multicolored lights. Most of the shops already have their doors propped open, and each threshold offers a new scent, song, or sale. Seaside Books reeks of cinnamon, Bing Crosby's rich baritone pours out of Dottie's Diner, and an unlicensed cardboard cutout of Mariah Carey outside of Sole-ly Shoes exclaims, "All I want for Christmas is Shoes!"

Only Ebb and Flow is dark. The derelict facade of the café is obfuscated by metal scaffolding, shoring, and thick sheets of semi-opaque plastic that shudder violently whenever there's a particularly stiff breeze. The susurrus of the passers-by is far louder. *The owner is either a drunk or a moron,* they wager, *who put the car in drive rather than in reverse. Or perhaps it's an insurance scam—did you know it was recently set on fire, too?*

A small handmade sign on the door reads: "Ebb and Flow is under construction. Visit Ebb and Flow 2 Go on Jefferson Court. Thanks a latte!" I should head there myself, but I remain rooted to the sidewalk like a weed sprouting between the cracks. The scuff of my tire tread is still visible on the curb. I hadn't hesitated after all.

I have been inside the café only once since the crash. It smells stale, like the inside of an empty refrigerator. The front of the building has been completely gutted. The ceilings are little more than exposed ductwork and wiring. The only remnant of furniture is the counter, covered in a heavy tarp. The floor is swept clean, albeit stained by something brown. I'm still not sure if it's oil from my Camry, spilled coffee, or Leigh's blood.

If I stand very still and concentrate very hard, I can see Ebb and Flow as it should have been. I would have set up the a-frame on the sidewalk, advertising seasonal desserts like chocolate bark topped with crushed peppermint, cookies made to resemble Santa Claus, and handmade marshmallows drizzled in white chocolate. The bell over the door would tinkle merrily as customers meandered in, and the heater would warm their pink-tipped noses. "Welcome to Ebb and Flow," we'd say, wearing crimson aprons with candy canes stashed in the pockets for the kids. "What can I get you?" We'd invite Wilson Ellicott, the town Santa, to sit by the electric fireplace and read stories. This year, Ebb and Flow is operating out of a converted Volkswagen Westfalia bus. The menu is limited to what Emmanuel can carry from his home kitchen. When Renee hung a strand of dollar store Christmas lights, I took them down. I don't feel like celebrating this year.

My phone chirps in my back pocket, but I don't bother looking at it. It'll undoubtedly be Renee, admonishing me for being late. Still, it does the trick—I continue on my way. Jefferson Court is just off Main, and it houses many of the more popular restaurants and bars in Wharton. If it were summertime, our location in the Swirly's parking lot would be a boon. But now, the ice cream shoppe is closed for the season. Most of the restaurants on Jefferson Court are closed for the season too, opening satellite locations in the more prosperous city of Norfolk.

The parking lot is deserted, save for Renee's pickup and an unfamiliar sedan. For a few weeks after we relocated, our more loyal customers would doggedly make the journey to order their usual and discreetly slot a few extra dollars into the tip jar. It's what we small-town folk do in a crisis — we band together, disguising aid as everyday routine so that no one feels unduly embarrassed. But when it got chillier, most chose to get their coffee from Dottie's Diner rather than making the trek out this way. I don't blame them. The eponymous Dottie always has a welcoming smile and a warm embrace for her regulars. I barely look up from the milk frother.

"Hey Renee," I say as I climb into the bus. With the space heater, countertop convection oven, and coffee urn inside, it is inordinately hot. Sweat prickles beneath my arms before I can even pull my apron over my head.

"Thank god, Hunter," Renee exclaims. "Did you read my text?" She pops up from her stool, flapping her arms like a flightless bird. Her signature oversized hoodie lends itself to the image.

"Yeah," I lie, "I'm sorry I'm late."

"He's been sitting out there since I opened," Renee babbles, clearly not concerned with my tardiness. "It's fucking creepy."

"Who?"

Renee leans out of the customer service window and jabs her finger at the sedan parked several spaces away from her own pickup. From here, it's apparent that someone is sitting in the driver's seat, and exhaust puffs out of the idling car's tailpipe. I can faintly hear the rumble of the engine. "I thought about just locking up, but I was too afraid to walk to my truck after," Renee continues. "I don't want to be featured on *Dateline*."

As we watch, the sedan's door opens, and a man steps out. He looks normal enough—wearing a sports coat, a polo stretched over a thick midsection, and pressed khakis. He casually tosses a McDonald's cup in the nearby trash can, and meanders in our direction, his hands shoved in his pockets. As he approaches the window, I can hear his keys—or perhaps loose change—jangling in his pocket. Despite being safely ensconced inside the bus, Renee ducks behind me. "Hello sir," I say, "what can I get you?"

The man doesn't answer. Instead, he pats at his sports coat, searching for something. *A gun, perhaps.* Renee's nervousness is rubbing off on me. Eventually, he finds what he's looking for: a small, spiral notepad. He flips through several pages, squints, then feels around in his jacket again. This time, he produces a pair of wire-rimmed glasses, which he slips over his ears. "'Hunter Bailey'?" he reads from the pad.

"Yes?"

"I'm Det—" He sighs and feels around in his jacket for a third time. Then, he pats his pants pockets. "I'm Detective Acker," he finally says, producing a police badge from his back pocket. "We're tying up loose ends on your case, and I was hoping for a few minutes of your time."

The phrase "your case" makes me feel uneasy. Still, I plaster on my very best customer service smile. "Sure thing, when would you like to do that? I'm at work, so maybe we could make an appointment sometime later in the week?"

Detective Acker looks around the vacant parking lot. His bristly mustache twitches, as if trying to contain a smile. "It doesn't look as though you're busy now." He gestures toward the unoccupied picnic bench we set up for customers. "As I said: it'll only take a few minutes."

Someone carved a heart into the bench of the picnic table. I idly trace the deep grooves with my finger. Renee places two paper cups in cardboard sleeves on the table for the detective and myself. "Two black coffees," she chirps before heading back to the bus.

Detective Acker pries the lid off, adding the contents of two pink sugar packets. He's unfazed by my fidgeting, humming as he stirs. Finally, he replaces the lid, taking a measured sip. "Great coffee," he says.

"Thank you," I mumble, curling my hands around my own warm cup.

"You've got a nice little operation goin' here," he says, tipping his chin in the direction of the Westfalia bus. Despite myself, I turn to look. The light emanating from the customer service window is warm and inviting, and inside, Renee bustles, her ponytail bouncing. The burr mill switches on, its distinctive *bzzz* drifting through the empty parking lot, followed by the nutty aroma of ground coffee.

"Thank you," I repeat.

Detective Acker reaches inside his sports coat pulling out a pen. "In your initial interview on the scene, you said that your car experienced brake failure. Is that correct?"

"Yes." My sandpaper tongue sticks to the roof of my mouth, and I take a swig of my coffee. It's the truth—at least, in part. Angus cut the brake line before the police arrived. "The brake line corroded."

The detective's mustache twitches. I can't tell if he's suppressing a smile or a sneeze. "Funny you say that because there was no sign of corrosion. The coating on the line wasn't abraded."

"I'm not a mechanic. That's just what I was told." The coffee sloshes in my stomach. I stepped right into that trap. "Maybe I misunderstood."

"Y'know, I drove past the café today," Detective Acker muses, "and you'd have to veer off Main Street to drive through the window. Pop up on the curb and everything."

"I panicked." *I'm panicking.* My heart is beating in my ears. I should have called my lawyer. "I didn't want to crash into a car."

Stop talking, Hunter!

"So in order to avoid a little fender bender, you caused $150,000 in property damage?" He rests his forearms on the tabletop. "Are you fucking kidding?"

"No sir," I mumble, picking at the cardboard sleeve on my cup. I can feel the proverbial snare tightening. It is a garrote around my neck, the wire sawing into my skin. "Can I call my lawyer?"

"Do you need to?"

"No, but—" I press my lips together, unsure. If I say "yes, I'd like to call her," then I'll look as though I have something to hide. Even if he does believe I crashed intentionally, he can't possibly discern why. Angus, Haley, and Candy along with Leigh's body were long gone before the police arrived. There was no trace of them left in the café except for the brown stain that may have been motor oil.

"I should call her," I say, fishing my cellphone out of my pocket. I unlock the screen, scrolling through the contacts for Eileen Choi, my business attorney. I'm not entirely sure she can help me, but she is the only lawyer I know.

"Do you know what I think, Mr. Bailey?" Detective Acker asks, snapping his notepad shut. "I think there's more to this than you're letting on."

My thumb hovers over the "call" icon, Eileen's headshot smiling at me. I shake my head but keep my mouth shut. I'm pleading the fifth until I speak to Eileen. I shouldn't have agreed to speak to him at all.

Detective Acker takes a gulp of his sweetened coffee, then licks at his lips. "I think that this has something to do with Angus Chilton."

I feel as though the bench tilts beneath me. "Excuse me? What did you say?"

"Last week, I received a call from the Portland Police Department about your ... friend." He spits the last word, his nose wrinkling disdainfully. "He's a person of interest in a murder investigation. Apparently, he's been extremely hard to locate. It's quite the coincidence, isn't it?"

"I'm not following."

"I was looking through the records. In the last eighteen months, we have been called out to Ebb and Flow *three* times." He counts them out on his fingers. "First, for the attempted murder of Mr. Chilton. Second, arson. And then, third, your supposed brake failure."

"I've had bad luck." I glance around the lot, desperate for any excuse to end this conversation. A woman walking a large German Shepherd eyes the Ebb and Flow 2 Go signage on the sidewalk ("New Location, Same Love") but doesn't enter the lot. Instead, her dog lifts his leg, soaking the corner of the a-frame chalkboard. The "-ve" in "love" liquifies, becoming a pink smear. "'Same lo,'" I mumble. "That sounds about right."

When Angus walked into my café, chaos swept through the door behind him. His promise to keep me safe wasn't a lie so much as an impossibility. My human body is just too fragile; I could tear apart as easily as a paper doll in the hands of an overzealous toddler. I've stood between warring wolves, and it was like facing off against titans. I wanted to be on equal footing, but instead, I was tripped and left out in the cold.

"Was Mr. Chilton with you when you crashed?" Detective Acker asks.

"No," I lie, "he was at home, asleep. It was very early in the morning."

"Interesting," the detective murmurs but doesn't elaborate. He gulps the last of his coffee, his Adam's apple bobbing. He crushes the cup in his hand, tossing it on the tabletop. It skitters, bumping into my mostly full cup. "Well, I'll get out of your hair," he says, stretching. "Throw that away for me, will you?"

"Sure," I say, relieved. The trash can is closer to him than to me, but I'm not about to complain. I'll gladly throw away his trash if he leaves.

Detective Acker stands and steps backward over the bench seat. He stuffs his notebook and pen back into his pocket. "I'd like to talk to Mr. Chilton. Is he home now?"

The question is like a knife through my ribs. Angus hasn't been home in weeks. Instead, I am haunted by his mail, his toothbrush sitting by the sink, and his clothes hanging in my closet. It's as though he's a ghost. Sometimes, when I sit on the couch, I inadvertently find myself in the divot made by his behind. Or I'll roll onto his side of the bed, the scent of his shampoo on the pillow rousing me. *Oh Angus, did you come home?* "He doesn't live with me anymore."

Detective Acker's eyebrows converge upon his hairline. "Interesting. Have a good day, Mr. Bailey."

I don't move from my seat until he gets into his car. I'm afraid I'll act in a peculiar way—move too stiffly, grin when I'm meant to look dour—and he'll be all the more suspicious. He waves out of the window at me as he pulls out of the lot, but I don't return the gesture. When he turns onto Jefferson Court and out of sight, I wake my phone. Eileen's contact information is still up, but I swipe back to the contacts screen, tapping on the name just above hers.

CHAPTER 5
(HENRY)

⊲◆⊳

Sevierville, Tennessee – July 1970

The basement of St. Cyprian's is drafty. When it is blustery outside, like today, the hopper windows rattle furiously. It makes it difficult to concentrate on Father Ricci's homily. Even with a congregation of one, he speaks with the fervor of a shepherd herding a flock one hundred strong. "Henry Lee, your daddy tells me you do not trust in the armor he has gifted you."

I kick at the tuffet folded into the pew, causing the hinges to clatter noisily. I can't sit still, desperate to be dismissed. It's a perfect day to fly a kite, and I don't want to waste it. I rub my fingers over the pockmarked bench. Someone scratched a Petrine cross into the polished wood with a pocketknife. Perhaps that's why this pew has been relegated to the basement with the dusty old books and the old baptismal fount.

I imagine a golden suit of armor with broad pauldrons and a plumed helmet. How could I be frightened of anything in that get up? Though, Father Ricci never says what he means. He takes great pleasure in scattering breadcrumbs, forcing his supplicants to beg for a mouthful. "What do you mean?" I ask.

"Your dad tried to teach you to shoot so that you could do the Lord's work, but you acted like a child." I don't bother reminding him that I *am* a child. It's as plain as day, and if he can't see it, then perhaps he needs glasses.

"I didn't like it," I say, tracing the inverted cross graffiti with my index finger. "It was too loud." I don't tell him that my father's enthusiasm frightened me. His hands shook as he slotted the bullets into the chamber, giving each a virtuous name: charity, chastity, verity, amity, and faith. When he demonstrated the proper posture, his fingers were like pincers, leaving purple blotches on my skin.

"We must be exuberant," Father Ricci says, "so that our message is clear."

"But—" I press my lips together, uncertain. The question lingers on the back of my tongue, unsaid.

"What is it, my child?" Father Ricci sits in the pew beside me, smoothing his cassock. He smells like pine and stale cigar smoke. I didn't know men of the cloth were allowed to smoke, though perhaps I'm thinking of monks.

"How can we tell if someone is good or evil?" I ask meekly, steeling myself for a stern rebuff. But the priest only laughs, clapping me on the shoulder. His laugh is boisterous, but I don't get the impression it's at my expense. It lacks the inherent cruelty of my father's laugh, which cuts to the bone.

"Come with me," Father Ricci urges. "Let's take a walk." On our way out of the basement, he stops to grab a canvas backpack. Something inside rattles.

St. Cyprian's is a blight on the nose of the beautiful Mater Dolorosa Cemetery. It's a small, wooden church, cruciform in shape. In disrepair for the better part of a decade, most of the shakes have fallen off the peaked roof, revealing the wooden sheathing and metal flashings underneath. Most of my friends attend the newer church on Primula Avenue because there's less likelihood of a roof leak during communion. With today's windstorm, I expect shingles to be flung miles away, leaving the roof as bald as Father Ricci's head.

It's been an unseasonably wet summer in Tennessee. The cemetery looks more like a swampland than a place of perpetual rest. The earth is slick and sloppy, filling my sneakers with muddy rainwater. While I slosh through it with the gangly gait of a colt, Father Ricci seems to float, his hands folded inside his sleeves. The near-constant rainfall has caused many of the older gravestones to tilt like a mouthful of crowded baby teeth. Some have fallen over entirely, and it's difficult to tell where the plots begin or end. The thought of inadvertently trodding upon someone's body makes me shudder. I imagine an achromic, desiccated hand bursting from the soil and snagging my ankle.

We walk the grounds in silence. I convince myself that Father Ricci forgot my question, but I don't dare ask again. Instead, I read the surnames carved into the tombstones. I find a Fairbanks and wonder if they are a relative of mine. I'm doubly careful not to walk on their plot where the ground is as spongy as peat.

Climbing the hill, we pass a mausoleum, which resembles a Grecian temple except in miniature. It's the only mausoleum at Mater Dolorosa, and its ostentatiousness causes it to stick out like a sore thumb. The only clue to the mausoleum's occupant is the name "Blake" carved just beneath the gable. No one is sure whether Blake is a surname or given name, nor can anyone recall when exactly the mausoleum was built. Naturally, stories abound, consisting of half-truths, legend, and lies. My friend Eddie thinks that Blake is a vampire.

When we reach the wrought iron gate, each picket capped with a fleur de lis, Father Ricci finally deigns to speak. "I think that, as men of God, we walk a very narrow path. We must point our feet toward goodness, like the Bible says, and turn our back toward evil. But evil can look a lot like goodness."

"Like Samuel?" I ask, referring to my stepfather. No matter how much I squint, I can't seem to see the horns upon his brow or the pitchfork hidden behind his back.

"Yes, like him." We walk along the fence line, fleur de lis shaped shadows dappling our path. My English teacher says that the fleur de lis is meant to resemble a lily, but I think they look more like a fool's cap.

I stop to pick up a stick, dragging it along the pickets. "Father Ricci," I manage, chewing at my lower lip. "Can someone be good but act evil?" It's a question that has been troubling me for some time.

The priest gives me a sidelong look. "Who are you referring to?"

The oldest section of the cemetery is shrouded in shadow, concealed amidst a copse of sweetgum trees.

The graves are far apart, weathered by the unrelenting seasons. Many of the stones cover interred Confederate soldiers, struck down in the Battle of Fort Sanders. The trees block the wind somewhat, and Father Ricci stops here, dropping the backpack on the ground. I scuff at the dirt with my sneakers. "My dad," I finally answer.

"Hmm," Father Ricci hums. To my relief, he doesn't seem angry. The priest spends a lot of time with my father, and I expect they are friends. Though, I've never known my father to have a friend, much less keep one.

Father Ricci kneels in the litterfall, unzipping the backpack. He fishes out a can of Del Monte fruit cocktail and sets it on the squarish top of a nearby gravestone. "Milton has a lot of anger inside of him," he replies, "and it gives the devil a foothold. But he is a pious man, and he knows where his faults lie."

There's nothing comforting about his answer—not really. It sounds like an excuse to handle my father with kid gloves, no matter what sin he commits.

Father Ricci pulls a small pistol out of the backpack, checking the chamber with practiced hands. In his past life, he must have been a soldier, though I can't picture him in anything other than a cassock. Gripping the weapon by its barrel, he offers it to me, grip-first. I hesitate. "C'mon," Father Ricci urges. "You need to practice, don't you?"

The pistol is heavy in my small hands. I look down the barrel at the Del Monte can, keenly aware that, with every inhale, the gun bobs. I hold my breath, puffing out my cheeks. "Don't hold your breath,"

Father Ricci says, "you'll pass out. When you exhale, squeeze the trigger."

"Okay." I do as he says. The gunshot is louder than I expect, not unlike the warning bark of a dog before it bites. I miss the can entirely. Instead, I hit the trunk of a sweetgum tree just to the left of the can. Father Ricci pries the bullet from the bark with his fingernail, tucking it into his pocket. I steel myself for a red-faced tirade, but it doesn't come. Father Ricci isn't my father.

"Try again," Father Ricci says encouragingly.

I aim at the can, listening to the wind ruffle the sweetgum's leaves. I aim for the center of the red Del Monte logo, smack dab between the L and M. *Bang!* The recoil burns my palms. Fruit juice pours out of the punctured can. Father Ricci whoops as though I just hit a home run. He scoops up the can, stuffs his fingers inside the borehole to select a cherry, and pops it into his mouth. He holds the can out to me, but I shake my head.

I hold the gun loosely at my side. I desperately want to put it down, but Father Ricci is pulling a pork bean can from the backpack. "Again," he says, placing it on the gravestone.

"Can … can I ask you another question?" I ask, as I take aim. The wind tousles my hair and I wait, my stance wide like John Wayne in a standoff.

"Sure," Father Ricci says, slurping juice from the punctured can. A dribble wets his clerical collar.

"Will it … make me a sinner? Will I go to Hell?" I squeeze the trigger and beans explode from the can. The tomato sauce oozes, dripping down the gravestone like blood. When it comes to "it," I don't elucidate.

Even thinking about it makes my stomach roil, and if I say it aloud, I'll surely vomit.

"I think that God can tell the difference between murder and purification, don't you?"

That night, I lie awake mulling over that very question. There's a flaw in the priest's logic, but he can't see it. How could he? As a man of the cloth, having faith is as autonomic as breathing. He bathes in it each time he mounts the pulpit, reading aloud from the book he's memorized since seminary. But I don't have faith—not even a little.

Surely, God knows that too.

Ridgerton, Tennessee—Present Day

"You brought the money, right?"

Dr. Edwin McNair, with his sharp features and severe underbite, strongly resembles a ferret. He's slippery like one too, weaseling out of any trap that's ever been laid for him.

"Yeah, Eddie." I have to raise my voice over the caterwauling of his caged patients. "Do they ever stop barking?"

Eddie pauses in the middle of the aisle, looking around as if seeing the rows of kennels for the first time. A large Doberman lunges at the bars, making his whole enclosure quake. Alarmed, I jump, but the veterinarian doesn't even flinch. "You know. I don't hear them after a while," he says serenely, sticking his fingers into the cage. The Doberman sniffs them excitedly, his whole body waggling. "My office is quieter."

Eddie leads the way into a small office, and when the door is shut, the barking becomes several decibels quieter. A large, locked cabinet and a refrigerator dominate the far wall. He motions to a hard plastic chair across from his desk, encouraging me to sit. "Where did I put my keys?" he mumbles to himself, pawing through his desk drawers. When he leans over, I catch a glimpse of the shiny bald spot on the top of his head, a few coarse hairs combed over it. I'm not sure why he doesn't just shave the rest. Perhaps it's vanity: a desire to cling to what once was. Hadn't he been voted "Best Hair" in our middle school yearbook?

While he searches, I examine the brochure rack. The glossy pamphlets run the gamut from heartworms to the dangers of declawing. I select one entitled "A Gentle Farewell," finding a sepia-toned image of a Golden Retriever and a mawkish poem about a rainbow bridge. I can't imagine Eddie comforting a grieving pet owner. He's too brash, too oafish. When I called him after my cat died, I remember him saying "them's the breaks" in his beat Mafioso impression. When I skinned my knee trying to pop a wheelie, he hawked a loogie on the pavement and solemnly said, "At least you didn't land on your fuckin' head, Fairbanks. You're ugly enough."

"Here it is," Eddie says, producing a key attached to a troll doll keychain. The troll's hair and belly button gem are neon green. Eddie unlocks the cabinet, revealing neatly stacked boxes emblazoned with cumbersome names like Zithromax, Methimazole, and Tramadol. He finds the box labeled Ketaset, setting it on his desk. "Should I ask what you need this for?"

Eddie asks warily. "You're not going to inject this into your dick or anything, right?"

"Should I ask you why you're willing to take a hundred bucks for it?" I counter.

Eddie winces. "Touché."

I toss the crumpled bill on the desk, and Eddie snatches it up as though it'll fly away. "How much do I need to sedate a dog?" I ask.

"What size is the dog?" Eddie sits behind his desk, tossing the troll doll keychain on top of the blotter. The ugly little creature—the troll, not Eddie—seems to stare through me. Its pupils are overly large, reminding me of my father's dilated eye when the wolf took his legs out from under him.

"Big," I say. "Damn near the size of a human." Eddie's eyebrow quirks, but he doesn't ask questions. That's the good thing about ole Eddie McNair: he knows when to mind his business.

"That's five milligrams per pound, injected in the muscle. There's five hundred milligrams in the vial, so as long as your dog is one hundred pounds, you'll be alright with one."

"Best give me a few more vials, Eddie. Some needles too."

I drive past the house three times.

The cookie-cutter homes in the gated community of Fox Glen are nearly indistinguishable from one another, with identical flat yards. At first glance, the mailboxes don't appear to have numbers on them, until

I realize the numbers are the same muted brown as the boxes themselves. Even with my glasses, I'm far too near-sighted to read them.

On my third trip down Oleander Terrace, all of the sprinklers activate one after another, trilling like cicadas. *Chhhrt, chhhrt, chht, chht!* Even though it is December, the lawns are verdant, devoid of dead leaves. I count three lawn care vans parked on this street alone, men with sun-reddened necks grappling against Mother Nature for another week of perfection. I roll my window down to ask one of the landscapers for directions to 133 Oleander.

"Three houses that way," the man drawls as he pulls a weed whacker out of the back of a *Green Dream Limited* van. "It's the one with the dogwood. We're goin' there next to yank that sonofabitch out o' the ground."

I pull into the drive of 133 Oleander. There is a dogwood tree in the yard, its dark branches devoid of greenery, flowers, or the clusters of oval-shaped fruit that we used to smush into "potions" as kids. Once, I smeared the potion on my sister's forehead, and she got a rash that was nearly as scarlet as the dogwood's berry. Someone spray-painted a red "x" on the tree's trunk, marking it for removal. It doesn't look particularly unhealthy, and the branches aren't infringing on the view. I can't imagine why they would cut it down.

Before getting out of the car, I pull a Ruger pistol out of my glove compartment, stashing it in the deep pocket of my windbreaker. Cordelia is my half-sister, but that's all the more reason to keep my guard up. We languished in the same womb, but we don't bleed the same blood. I imagine hers is coagulated and mucilaginous, as if exposed to haemotoxic venom. It's the sort of blood that would make a schlocky B-movie horror director cum in his pants.

The woman who answers the door does not look like the six-year-old I last saw when I was thirteen. Gone are the denim cutoffs and paisley peasant blouses tied just above the midriff. Instead, she wears culottes and a modest button-down. The Farrah Fawcett flick has been tamed into a sleek bob, prettily framing her face. "Yes? Can I help you?"

"It's me, Cordelia. Henry." I feel awkward. It's as though I'm talking to someone with a grotesque, oozing boil on their face. It's rude to make eye contact with the pustule or draw undue attention to it, but it's *there*, in your periphery, pulsing. Cordelia's demonic affliction is less conspicuous than a boil, but I can sense it. I put my hand in my pocket, finding the comforting chill of the pistol's handle.

"Henry?" She gasps. "What a surprise." She hesitates, her eyes flitting from side to side, but she steps aside so that I can come in.

The foyer has inordinately high ceilings, and my footsteps echo in a particularly unsettling way. I almost don't recognize my own voice when it bounces back. Perhaps it is the voice of Detective Dupin, manifested. "I'm sorry I didn't call first. I didn't have your number."

I nearly trip over the shoes by the front door. They aren't neatly lined up in pairs but strewn. It's a compelling tableau—delineating the inherent differences between my sister and me. Nature versus nurture. Growing up, she lived with our mom and Samuel full-time. At the farm, there was a mudroom that existed purely to store foul-smelling work boots. No one paid any mind as to whether a pair belonged to them or whether they were a matching set at all. If they fit, then they fit. Simple as that. Often, mom would go to gather the eggs at dawn, wearing a rubber rainboot and a winter boot lined with sheepskin.

Conversely, my father fussed when my Keds had a grass stain on them, and he would make me scrub them with Griffin shoe polish until the solvent burned all the hair out of my nostrils. I can't imagine how many Our Fathers I'd have to recite if they weren't placed properly on the shoe rack.

"I thought I would hear from you after dad died last month," Cordelia says, her arms crossed over her chest. It's not an accusation; there's a sadness there, a yearning that makes me want to laugh. She missed me!

Dad. She says it as though he belonged to both of us. But Samuel Campbell was her father, not mine. I don't bother reminding her. It'll only cause a fight, and I need information. "I came to the funeral."

"I didn't see you."

"Would you have recognized me, if you had? It's been fifty-three years, Cordy."

Cordelia softens at the nickname. "Come in," she says, ushering me into the living room. It's a dull-looking space, reminiscent of a furniture showroom. Black iron metalwork—"Family" written in bubbly cursive—hangs on the shiplapped wall, surrounded by framed photos of the aforementioned ménage. The camel-colored sectional Cordelia directs me to is ultramodern with stick-thin legs. I'm afraid to sit on it, fearing it'll collapse beneath my weight. Instead, I veer toward the photos.

"We took them in Rio de Janeiro last summer," Cordelia says. I can recognize some of the people in the photos, though they are all much older than I remember. There's Cordelia, in a white bikini and matching kimono. Her well-manicured hands rest on the handlebars of a beach wheelchair, its cartoonishly oversized wheels dwarfing the small man slumping in the seat. It is as though someone stuffed my stepfather into the dryer when his tag clearly said "lay flat." He's shrunk, his spine resembling a parenthesis. Working on a farm gave him weathered, blotchy skin, but old age was like an incessant hailstorm upon his features.

The other two are strangers. A man I presume is Cordelia's husband stands with his arm looped around her waist, smiling so hard his eyes are crinkly. He's sunburnt, the pale skin of his naked chest nearly Pepto-Bismol pink. A younger woman perches on the edge of a lounger, her face upturned toward the sky. Unlike the older set, she isn't wearing swimwear, opting for a pair of black cutoffs and a Led Zeppelin band tee.

Haley. I've never met her, though I saw the back of her head at Samuel's funeral. "You have a beautiful family." That's what you're supposed to say, isn't it?

"Thank you. Would you like a cup of coffee?" Cordelia asks. "I have some coffee cake too—Entenmann's."

"Yeah, sure," I mumble, even though coffee gives me heartburn. While she heads to the kitchen, I peruse the other photos. There's one of Cordelia and her husband dining at what appears to be a Michelin-starred restaurant, their place settings meticulously arranged with nearly twenty pieces of cutlery between them. She has her cloth napkin in her hand as if about to place it on her lap. His sunburn is still visible beneath the collar of his pressed shirt, the skin beginning to peel. I'm surprised the restaurant let him in. Weren't they worried about skin flakes garnishing the soup?

Another photo shows Haley standing in front of a tour bus. She's holding her phone up to her face, presumably photographing whoever was photographing her. I can just barely make out the upturned corner of her lip, the sharp point of her canine tooth. She looks for all the world like a typical young woman traveling with her family: aloof and a little bored but making do because at least she's summering in a tropical paradise. I lean close to the image, my breath fogging the glass.

Cordelia seems to materialize at my shoulder. I hadn't heard her come back into the room. "I forgot to ask: would you like anything in your coffee? I think I have a bit of caramel creamer in the fridge."

"Black is fine," I reply, taking the mug from her hand. "You have a beautiful daughter."

Cordelia looks at the photo with a sad smile. "Haley has had such a hard time since dad died." I think of Tara's leg, dumped into some dumpster with the rest of the medical waste. *A hard time is an understatement.*

My sister urges me to the couch again, and this time, I sit. She's placed two plates on the squat coffee table, a wedge of cake on each. I poke at the crumb topping with the tines of my fork. "Where is Haley living now? I would like to meet her."

"She's in Virginia," Cordelia says, sitting beside me. She cups her own coffee mug in both hands. "It was a surprise to us when she left. But she seems better there—lighter. We text sometimes."

"You said she took ... dad's death hard?" The word "dad" sits on my tongue like a pill I can't seem to swallow, the acidic medicine pooling. But Cordelia reacts just as I need her to. She relaxes and leans back into the couch cushions, taking a sip of coffee. I reminded her of our connection—that I'm not a stranger who wandered in off the street.

"Haley takes everything hard." Cordelia presses her lips together. The corners, untouched by her crimson lipstick, blanch. It makes her look like a corpse, dolled up for a viewing. When I first saw her, she didn't look like she was my age; I would have bet my bottom dollar she was in her late thirties. But now that we're sitting side-by-side, I can see the shallow crow's feet beneath her caked-on foundation, a few strands of silver, wiry hair at her temples.

"The Montanari curse." I chuckle, thinking of our mother, Nadia. She was always so hard on herself, too. When I left as a preteen, she sobbed, wailing, *What have I done?* It wasn't her fault, not really. Much stronger women than her have been seduced by demons.

"Henry." Cordelia places her coffee on the tabletop. "Can I ask why you're here? I haven't seen you in ... decades."

"I was in town for the funeral." I take a gulp of my coffee, wracking my brain for an excuse for why I'm here—why I've been gone so, so long. It's too hot, searing the lining of my throat. "I'm sorry," I cough. "I shouldn't have come."

"Oh, I don't mean it like that." Cordelia rests her hand on my knee. "I'm glad you're here. Can you stay for dinner? John, my husband, will be off work soon." Outside, a loud metallic whirring begins, followed by gnashing and spitting sounds. The landscapers must be cutting down the dogwood tree. "Thank goodness. That damn tree was dumping flowers all over in the fall. It cost so much to get them swept and hauled away."

"You used to think they were beautiful," I remark, thinking of the little girl who would spin beneath the flowering trees, pretending she was a faerie.

"Most things are beautiful when you're a child," Cordelia chuckles, "because you don't have to pick up the mess." I imagine Cordy doesn't realize what a mess our childhood actually was. Or was that just mine?

"Can I use your bathroom?" I ask abruptly.

"It's down the hall, third door on the right."

I set my mug and untouched cake carefully on the table, and I head down the hall. Clandestinely, I ease open closed doors, finding a neatly organized linen closet, a home office with a Peloton bike, and a bathroom that smells strongly of bleach. There are two other closed doors beyond the bathroom, and after a quick glance back the way I came, I investigate those, too.

The room across from the bathroom is the color of Hubba-Bubba bubble gum. The curtains are pink, the polka-dot wallpaper is pink, and the bedspread is pink too. When the door swings open, the papers on the corkboard rustle, drawing my attention. They are all pen drawings of anatomically flawed horses on college-ruled paper, clearly ripped directly from a spiral notebook. Each is sloppily signed by the artist: "Haley Campbell."

Stacked cardboard boxes line the walls. Keeping an ear out for my sister, I rifle through the nearest one, finding only clothes. The next is heavy, filled to the brim with textbooks with titles ranging from *An Introduction to Data Collection and Statistical Analysis* to *Abnormal Psychology*. Frustrated, I rifle through the bedside table drawer, finding a bottle of Tylenol, several hair ties, and a tin of Altoids that, on closer inspection, contains an eighth of marijuana.

Then, I notice the mattress. Something is wedged under the corner of the headboard, making it appear lumpy. I reach under it, pulling out a leatherbound diary tied with a cord. I only have to glance inside to recognize the writing and its cadence. It's the same blocky print that he used on every birthday card, "Happy birthday, champ!" I shove the book into my jacket pocket.

I've been gone for far too long. I plan to cross the hall to the bathroom to flush the toilet and run the tap, but when I leave Haley's room, I nearly run headlong into my sister. "Henry! What were you doing in there?" she asks, her brow furrowing. "That's … my daughter's room."

"I-I must have gotten turned around," I stammer.

She peers over my shoulder, looking for anything amiss. I had left the box full of clothes open, a sweater and a camisole on the floor. The drawer of the nightstand is still ajar. *Shit.*

"I knew I shouldn't have let you in my house," Cordelia says, fishing her cellphone out of her pocket. "You've always been fucking creepy."

A memory ricochets through me: *Cordelia twirls beneath the dogwood tree, the petals falling like a gentle springtime rain. She spins so fast that her skirt flares out, making her look like a courting bird of paradise. Her opaque tights are ripped at the knee, and the skin beneath is an angry, shiny red. She says she tripped when getting off the school bus, but she had been pushed. The other kids tease her because they are too afraid to tease me. I really should put her out of her misery. Her existence is painful, isn't it? How can she possibly be free sharing her body with a demon?*

"Where is Haley, Cordy?" I ask. "It's important."

"Get out of my house, or I'll call the cops," Cordelia snaps, jabbing her finger down the hall. "Don't come back."

"Cordelia—"

"I mean it." Cordelia dials 9-1-, but I slap the phone out of her hand. She stares at me, slack-jawed

"I'm sorry," I say, bouncing the back of her head off the doorframe like a basketball. "I'm really sorry." Unconscious, her legs crumple, and I guide her to the carpet despite the creaking of my own knees.

CHAPTER 6
(ANGUS)

———— ◁◆▷ ————

Sitting cross-legged on the floor, I sift through the ornament box. While some families organize their ornaments—nestling them in cut-up egg cartons or wrapping them in newspaper—the Chiltons just toss them into the box, loose. "This is a problem for future me," we'd say, laughing as though it's the funniest joke in the world. I'm paying for it now. Somehow, all of the hooks have come off the baubles, teardrops, and snowflakes.

I pull a beige, puck-shaped ornament from the box. It's made of salt dough, a tiny handprint pressed into the middle. On the back, someone had scratched "Angus, 1989." I have a hazy memory of Ama pressing my hand into the soft, malleable dough, singing along to "Christmas Time Is Here" as *A Charlie Brown Christmas* played on the television. Even though she told me not to, I licked my palm afterward, expecting the sugary sweetness of cookies.

My phone chimes on the coffee table, the screen illuminating. My lock screen is a photo of Hunter and

69

me on our back deck, both holding sweating glasses of Sauvignon Blanc. His chin rests on my shoulder, his eyes half-lidded like a content cat. I've tried to change the photo, but I can't quite work up the nerve. It feels too final, as though we're *over, over.* A second chime follows the first, both text notifications bearing Hunter's name. It's the first time he's texted in weeks.

[Hunter: We need to talk.]

[Hunter: Now.]

I don't want to seem too eager. Nor too interested.

[Angus: About?]

[Hunter: About NOT going to jail. Meet me at home.]

I set my phone aside, grinding the heels of my hands into my eye sockets. When the dark motes clear, I find Toby staring at me from her spot on the couch, a tangle of Christmas lights in her lap. She picks at the knots, gently coaxing them loose with her fingernails. Beside her, Ama snores softly, her chin tucked into her chest. She fell asleep midway through her mug of hot cocoa.

"It's Hunter," I whisper. "He wants to see me."

"That's good, right?" Toby asks, her voice low. "You've been at a stalemate for a while."

"I'll have to finish this later. I need to meet him at the house." I place the lid on the Rubbermaid container, shoving the whole lot into the corner. The ornaments inside clink together.

Toby presses her lips together. "But—"

"It's important, Tobe. We can finish the tree tonight." I retrieve my coat from the rack, slipping it on. "Make sure Ama eats something and takes her pills when she wakes up," I remind her. I step into my boots, not bothering to tie the laces.

"I'll try," Toby replies. "You know how she is." Ama hates when we make a fuss over her. Every offer to help is met with a snippy, *Stop mothering me!* Once, when I offered Ama my elbow so she could climb the rickety porch steps, she slapped my arm and shouted, "You can help me into my casket, Aggie!"

Outside, it is blustery. This close to the ocean, the wind whips, making my long hair lash against my cheeks. I duck my head, focusing on the gravel road beneath my boots. Above me, a seagull shrieks, its boomerang-shaped shadow darkening the quartzite. Hunter's text troubles me. Or rather, the fragments making up the message do; I can't quite discern how they fit together. What unsettles me most is the urgency of it. *Now.*

I haven't been to our bungalow in weeks, though I've driven by it plenty. Not one iota of it has changed. Even the coffee mug I'd inadvertently left on the wide arm of the Adirondack chair is still there, the sip of leftover coffee becoming sludgy and rancid. In my lowest moments, I see it as a taunt, as subtle as brickbat. *I'm not even thinking about you,* it seemed to say.

Hunter opens the door before I can ring the bell. It's a relief; I didn't want to experience the indignity of ringing the bell to enter my own house. Hunter is pale, his features drawn as if he hasn't eaten in days. He has a bad habit of subsisting on coffee when he's stressed, mistaking the sloshing in his belly for satiation. "Get inside," he says, stepping aside.

"What is going on?" Our foyer is narrow, forcing us to stand so close that I can feel his body heat. "Your text said—"

"I know what it said," he snaps, clearly already irritated with me. "There was a man waiting at the truck this morning. He introduced himself as Detective Acker from Wharton P.D. He said he was there to wrap up the investigation into my crash." He nearly chokes on the word "crash," as though the consonants scraped against his hard palate.

"Okay," I reply. "That's okay. We expected that, Hunt." I gently take his arm, propelling him into our living room; he doesn't shrug me off. Instead, he sinks onto the couch, amidst a pile of half-folded laundry.

"But he didn't just ask about that. He asked about you—and Portland."

A chill sweeps down my spine. I kneel so that Hunter and I are eye-to-eye, resting my hands on his bouncing knees. "What did he say, exactly?"

"Portland called the station. They told Acker that you were a person of interest in a murder investigation there. They want to talk to you—*Acker* wants to talk to you. He asked me if you were home, but I told him you didn't live here anymore." Hunter's pink tongue sweeps out from between his wind-chapped lips, wetting them.

"Fuck!" I snarl, jerking to my feet like a marionette whose strings have been tugged, I pace, chewing on the inside of my cheek. Since James' death, I've gotten reckless—I see that now. I let myself exist on paper, signing my name on a W-2. I may as well have constructed a neon sign above Wharton, a blinking arrow pointed at my house. Paresthesia prickles on the backs of my hands, and I clench them into fists. I want to punch a hole in the drywall.

"But you didn't do anything in Portland," Hunter murmurs. "Right?"

"That's the problem. I should have done some-thing—*anything*. Instead, I helped James cross state lines and let him hurt more people."

Hunter rubs the back of his neck. Even a year removed, the fibrous scars left by James' claws are still shiny, bright white against his freckled skin. He swallows hard, his Adam's apple bobbing. I know that, sometimes, he still dreams of the bonfire. "Can't you just tell them it was James?"

I laugh, but there's no humor in it. It sounds more like a bark, a croupy cough, a goose's honk. "When they ask where James is, what do I say? 'I murdered him and let his sister bury him somewhere between here and New Orleans. You want to talk to her? Do you happen to have a Ouija board?'"

Hunter scoffs. "I'm only asking. You don't have to be rude to me."

"I'm sorry," I say. "I just feel—"

"Sick? I know. I puked in the dumpster behind 2 Go after he left," Hunter admits. "Detective Acker also seems less than convinced my crash was an accident. He doesn't know why, but he thinks I did it on purpose. He also thinks you were there."

"It's my lucky day," I grumble. "I have to get back ho—I mean, to Ama's." I imagine the detective sitting on Ama's couch with his knees wide, asking about me. I imagine him using my absence as a way to take advantage of the situation, twisting Ama's words until she's trussed up in them. She's nowhere near senile, but she's not exactly clear-headed either, especially after she takes her anticholinergic medication.

"Angus, wait—" Hunter rises from the couch, snagging my wrist. When I meet his eyes, he releases me, his shoulders slumping. His mouth opens and closes like a fish out of water. "Please be careful," he finally says.

II. December

CHAPTER 7
(HUNTER)

◁◆▷

*I*t's a blustery day, even the clouds look windswept. *They are stretched thin, resembling spun sugar. The wind whips off of the sea foam, raking its fingers through my hair. The chill slaps at my cheeks like a spurned lover in a telenovela. Still, I sit on the narrow stretch of sand in Tranquil Cove, watching the colorful buoys bob atop the cresting waves. There is a myriad of colors and patterns—red, green, blue, yellow striped, black polka-dot—each corresponding to a lobster boat. Crab traps are a commodity, and lord help the person who takes a bounty from another fisherman's trap. When I was a child, my mother told me the variegated buoys belonged to the mermaids who lived in the cove.*

The ocean churns, thickening the spume. Aphrodite was born of sea foam, wasn't she? Perhaps it happened on a day like this one, the water bubbling like soup on a stovetop. Suddenly, one by one, the buoys disappear into the drink. Pop, pop, pop, pop! I clamber to my feet to get a better view, brushing sand off of my jeans. Cupping my hands around my eyes like binoculars, I stare at the horizon, expecting them to shoot back to the surface. Perhaps the lines were tugged by a dolphin, plundering the traps, except I don't spot the telltale dorsal fin or the eddy of sputum jettisoned from a blowhole.

Abruptly, the breakers retreat, revealing a swath of silken, water-logged sand. It has the viscosity of quicksand, sucking at my heels. A group of ghost crabs converge on a sea nettle, beached by the sudden low tide. I find myself wondering if they appreciate the sting much like humans appreciate spice.

A chill sweeps down my spine as the water withdraws well past the cove's narrow mouth. Seagulls circle the newly-revealed tide pools—or rather, puddles—looking for a tasty morsel. Sunlight bounces off the scales of flopping fish, unable to breathe in the inch of water now suddenly allotted to them. "A tsunami," I breathe.

Living this close to the ocean, certain rules were ingrained in me. When caught in a rip current, swim parallel to the shore. Keep an eye out for sharks and storm clouds. If the tide changes suddenly, run and seek higher ground—or die. I want to run, but the viscous sand holds fast to the soles of my feet. I heave but only succeed in falling to my knees. The sand swallows my lower legs with a wet burp. I flop, not unlike the dying fish. "Help!" I scream, digging my fingers into the sand, trying, in vain, to pull myself free. "Someone help me!"

I'm wasting my energy. The nearest parking lot is a mile away, and it's unlikely anyone is on the trail leading to this little slice of beach. It's an oft-overlooked offshoot of the main footpath—an easier hike promising a cliffside photo op, picnic area, and playground. When the roar of the approaching wave hammers my eardrums, I fall upon the sand, spent. A cast of crabs side-step past me, their claws raised as if excited. Perhaps they are. Wharton will be their domain when it is underwater.

I should close my eyes and hold my breath. Instead, I look toward the roaring, wanting to see the hammer coming to strike me down, except there's no water. Instead, an enormous wolf strides across the sand, leaving massive footprints behind. It's the color of sea foam—a dingy white—with ribbons of kelp tangled in its damp fur. It smells rank, like butyric acid: wet dog and stomach acid. Its eyes are blue.

Angus?

I try to sit up, but the sand holds me fast. The wolf towers over me, standing to its full height on its muscular haunches. The freight train roar blares. The wolf's tongue lolls out of its mouth, saliva dripping onto my prone body.

"This is what you want?" Angus asks, tugging at the fur on his deep chest. I can't answer him because I can't hear myself think. I'm not entirely sure how I can hear him over the din. It's as though his voice is booming inside my skull. "Don't say I didn't warn you." With that, he digs his claws into the divot beneath his sternum, pulling away the layers of flesh, muscle, and fat. Blood, still warm, splatters upon me like rain.

My throat sears, and I realize I am screaming; my larynx and arytenoids shred like crepe paper. "Angus, no! Stop!"

Angus doesn't seem to hear me. He moves his hands as if removing a button-down, but instead, he pries open his ribs and clavicle, revealing the organs beneath the cage of bone. Unceremoniously, he rips out his lungs and heart, tossing them onto the beach. His heart beats for a moment longer, leaking watery, pinkish fluid onto the sand. Bizarrely, Angus seems unaffected by his missing organs or the latticework of his ribcage jutting out of his body. "You asked for this," he reminds me.

"Not this! Jesus, Angus! Not this!" The wolf grasps me by the waist, holding me at arm's length like a child examining a new doll. I feel so small; his paws are the size of platters. I stare into the chasm of his chest. Without his organs, the paraspinal muscles and the stack of vertebrae are plainly visible.

Angus tucks me inside his chest cavity with the same care with which a surgeon would transplant a heart. The impossibility of my imprisonment doesn't even cross my mind. I am only keenly aware of my bones breaking as I am tamped down into the cramped space. Angus shuts his ribcage, locking me in. Then, he adjusts his skin, leaving me in the dark. "Isn't this what you wanted, Hunter? To be just like me?"

I can't breathe. I pound against Angus' chest wall, kicking at the nearest rib until the costal cartilage splinters, violently ripping it from the sternum. Angus just snickers, making me tumble head over foot. "This is what you wanted," he repeats. "Now you can feel just like me."

Suddenly, I am inundated with violent sights and smells: the taste of venison, pungent steam rising from the animal's innards; a naked man grinding atop Angus' hips, molting antlers adhered to his furrowed brow; the searing pain of a broken jaw and the insufferable itch of healing skin. I cannot discern if they are memories or nightmares—they tangle together, forming a violent tableau.

I bolt upright, fighting my comforter as though it's the nightmare wolf's ribcage. The thin, cotton sheet beneath it tangles around my bare legs, and I fall out of bed in my haste to free myself. *Oomph.* Ghost hops off my bookshelf to come sniff me, his tail puffed up in alarm.

The details of my Cronenbergian nightmare dwindle as I disentangle myself from my damp sheets and stumble to the bathroom. It's very late—or very early. The only light penetrating the skylight is from the neighbor's floodlight, which clicks on whenever a breeze rustles the shrubs flanking the property line. I've asked him to angle it away from my windows countless times, but he just mumbles about the shadow creature he saw skulking around the autumn before last. "I swear, Mr. Bailey, it slithered through y'er kitchen window!"

Opening the medicine cabinet, I shake three tablets from the Excedrin bottle, placing them on my tongue. I tilt my head beneath the faucet, sloppily swallowing the pills and a mouthful of chlorinated tap water. My reflection in the mirror is blurry; I wipe the crust from my eyes with my knuckles, blinking rapidly. I am struck by how old I appear. Part of it is the sleeplessness and the unforgiving winter bluster, but I look as though I've aged a decade. I frown, the movement causing my overly chapped lips to crack. I've lost weight. There are deep hollows above my collarbones, and my sternum juts out of my skin like a pop-up timer out of a turkey. Ding! I'm done.

My watch vibrates, letting me know it's 4:30 a.m. It's time to get ready for work. I'm relieved. I didn't want to climb back into bed; it would feel performative to toss and turn, knowing I'll white-knuckle the comforter rather than closing my eyes. I can't stomach the thought of stumbling into another nightmare.

I turn on the shower before stepping out of my boxer briefs, kicking them into the hamper. I've been neglecting laundry, and the peak juts out of the basket. It sways precariously when the underwear lands on the summit but doesn't fall. I can go another day without lugging it down the hall to the washing machine. The shower is too hot, but I don't turn down the temperature. The reddening of my skin feels therapeutic, somehow; perhaps, it will all slough off, and I will be born anew.

As I wash, the movements mechanized, I find myself thinking about the nightmare that woke me. The images that flashed through my head after I was forcibly joined with Angus were both gluttonous and pornographic. Sex and sustenance ignited the same synapse in his head. Despite the heat beating against my back, gooseflesh prickles on my arms. When we made love, did Angus think of me as food? Perhaps, for him, love is fleeting, leaving him with a bloated belly and a wandering eye. After all, one meal can't sustain a body for very long.

It's unseasonably warm for the first of December. I take off my coat as soon as I arrive at the bus, draping it over the edge of the basin sink. I hate days like this, which we Virginians dub "false Spring." They are sprinkled throughout the winter months, spaced far enough apart to give us hope that warmer weather is imminent. It's far more likely that tomorrow will be blisteringly cold.

"Hey boss," Haley says breathlessly, pushing down the plunger on the French press. Her bangs stick to her forehead. She's frazzled, not altogether familiar with the menu. She's only been working for me for a few weeks. The binder with drink recipes lies open on the countertop, a bit of chocolate drizzle staining the dog-eared page—and her cheek.

I stand on my tiptoes to turn on the oscillating fan. A meager breeze sweeps through the bus, rustling our hair. "How's business?" I ask, retrieving my tote bag from the doorway. It's heavy, filled with cans of evaporated milk, coffee filters, and sachets of meat and cheese. I've been neglecting the shopping, much like my laundry.

Haley pours the coffee into a paper cup, leaning out the window to hand it to a waiting patron. For the first time in quite a while, there's a staggered line outside, five people deep. Most wear their coats open or over their arms, beanies stuffed into pockets. "Busy," Haley manages, already scooping ice into a plastic cup for the next customer. "I didn't expect to open alone this morning."

"I didn't expect anyone to be here," I admit. "We've barely had a customer in weeks." I plaster on my best customer service facade, finding my muscles inelastic and uncooperative. It takes more muscles to frown than smile, the old adage says, but I'm not sure I agree. "What can I get you?" I ask a woman with a short, blond bob, the bangs made crispy by hairspray.

"Do you do frappuccinos?" the woman asks, wrinkling her nose at the chalkboard menu. "I don't see them here."

"We don't. We have an iced coffee, and I can put whip and whatever swirl you'd like on it. We have chocolate and caramel." I can't hide the ennui in my voice. This certainly isn't the first time I've had this conversation. Hell, it's not the first time *this week,* and it's only Tuesday.

"But I want a mocha cookie crumble frappuccino," she says slowly. "Like they have at Starbucks." Her lower lip juts out as if she's a baby about to have a tantrum.

"Ma'am, this isn't a Starbucks," I deadpan. "There's one out on Route 50."

"But you're here," the woman says, crossing her arms over her chest. "Can't you make one?"

"I can do an iced coffee, as I've mentioned. It's plenty sweet." I lean close as though we are sharing a secret. "You're in luck because I'm very heavy-handed with the whipped cream."

"But—"

"Jesus, lady," Haley groans, delivering an iced coffee and a parchment paper-wrapped sandwich to a man waiting at the pickup counter. "We don't have your overpriced milkshake here, okay? You're holding up the line."

I duck my head, coughing into my fist to hide my guffaw.

The woman huffs, her cheeks reddening. She opens and closes her mouth like a fish out of water. "They would never talk to their customers like this at Starbucks!" she finally says. "I'll be writing a Yelp review just as soon as I get home!"

Haley slaps her palms on the countertop. "Good! Then all of the internet will know that you can't read a fucking menu!" The woman stomps toward her car, her shoulders so stiff they touch her ears. Her purse swings from her fist, nearly striking the other patrons who watch the altercation with a certain bored detachment. A few smile, shaking their heads as if to say, *One less person in line.*

"Who's next?" Haley barks.

While she takes an order—coffee, hot—I pour from the carafe, popping on the lid with practiced fingers. Working in tandem, we clear the line with no more hiccups. It feels good to empty my head of the anxious static, swaddling myself in familiarity. I inhale the scent of ground coffee, finding comfort there. If I close my eyes, I can even pretend I'm inside Ebb and Flow proper rather than this oversized tin can.

The back door of the bus bangs open, and Emmanuel climbs the stairs, balancing a large tray on his palm. He moves with the fluid grace of a yogi, placing it on the narrow counter. "I have a delivery," he sing-songs. The buttery and yeasty aroma of croissants fills the space, making me salivate.

"You made these in your kitchenette?" I gasp, knowing the layered pastry can be quite time-consuming. Even in the commercial kitchen with its food prep table, industrial mixer, cooling racks, and other specialized accouterments, the finicky pastry can turn out too dense or as flat as a pancake if the baker looks at it too hard.

"Hunter, I used to bake cheesecake with Nilla Wafers, expired cream cheese, and a packet of Kool-Aid for color," he chuckles, referring to his decade-long stint in prison. "See if they can do that at Le Cordon Bleu."

"You're a miracle worker." I clap him warmly on the shoulder. If I am this café's heart, Emmanuel is its soul. It's apparent in every perfect croissant, the fine-lined icing ringing the sugar cookies he prepares for every holiday.

Emmanuel just shrugs, unwrapping a stick of Nicorette gum. "Did that private dickhead come by here?"

I select a croissant from the tray, nibbling the end. "Who do you mean?"

"The detective," Emmanuel says, chewing noisily. "He knocked on my door, shouting questions 'bout the bad luck at the café. I told him to come back with a fuckin' warrant, that if he burnt my croissants by distractin' me, I'd send an invoice to Wharton P.D."

I choke on the bit of pastry, swiping at my mouth as if it'll dislodge it from my windpipe. Haley thumps me on the back until I spit it onto the floor. My stomach is a greasy mire. I peer out into the lot as if expecting to see the detective's sedan idling there. But it's empty now, the only movement a crumpled napkin skittering across the pavement.

CHAPTER 8
(HENRY)

◁◆▷

Wharton, Virginia—July 1970

In the mirror, marred by hundreds of fingerprints, my face looks as though it's made of silly putty; it's been stretched wide, my ears protruding like Dumbo's. I open and close my mouth, examining my teeth. I chipped the incisor playing soccer in the house, smacking my chin on the coffee table after a particularly wild kick. Now, the chip looks as deep as the grand canyon, or rather, how deep I imagine the Grand Canyon to be. I've never seen it except in books.

My mother laughs at my reflection, sticking out her tongue. "Shall we go get some ice cream?" she asks, mussing my hair. In the mirror, I can see a woman in a bikini top and linen pedal pushers admiring herself in the mirror opposite. It makes her look inordinately statuesque and stick thin. She props her hand on her hip, turning this way and that. I've never seen a girl wearing so little—girls don't dress like that in

Sevierville. My father was right: this is a hotbed of debauchery and sin.

"Can I get rainbow sprinkles?" I ask, tearing my eyes away. I try to focus on the bizarro version of me, opening my mouth to stare at my uvula.

"Of course, darling. But first, we have to get through the maze! Will you lead the way?" my mother says. Puffed up with an inflated sense of importance, I lead her through the mirror maze and back out into the sunlight. Samuel is waiting for us there, his big hands resting on the handlebar of my sister's stroller.

"How was it?" he asks. The tip of his nose is sun-reddened.

Even when I expect to see him, it is still very much akin to watching the scene in *The Thing* where the creature is immolated, the flames burning so brightly it blew out the film. It's a shock to the system, twanging the synapses that activate fight or flight. I think of looking at him through the crosshairs, trying to slow the staccato of my rabbit-heart. I imagine being brave enough to squeeze the trigger, the recoil of the rifle butting against my shoulder. Would he have splintered apart, revealing a mess of maggots and gelatinous goo inside? Surely, the devil won't have organs like a normal man, all neatly tucked into their respective places!

"It was lovely, wasn't it, Henry?" My mother asks, giving my narrow shoulders a shake. "Henry was very brave. Shall we go to the ice cream shop before we meet the Chiltons? I promised a certain little man some sprinkles."

Samuel looks at me with his impossibly dark eyes. They crinkle at the corners, his lips spreading into a smile that shows all of his teeth. "Sure," he says, "I hope they have cherry-pineapple swirl."

Somewhere on Highway 58—Present Day

The truck stop is on a quiet part of the interstate, lit only by two functioning streetlights, or rather, one functioning light and another that flickers while making an alarming humming noise. The others are disabled; tweakers dug up the copper wire that connects the streetlights to the power grid and no one bothered to replace it. The shallow trenches remind me of burial plots. When I was a kid, we would play outside the gates of Mater Dolorosa Cemetery, watching the backhoe scoop up mounds of dirt. We would push each other toward the wrought iron gates, shouting dares to jump in. I was the only one who went through with it, lying in the dirt with my arms crossed over my chest until a gravedigger chased me away.

The bathroom is less hospitable than the parking lot. The lights are blue, to stop the aforementioned addicts from shooting up in the stalls. It's hard to find a vein when everything is the color of veins. The ambience gives me a headache, but it's far more preferable than listening to Cordelia's incessant shrieking from the trunk. Sitting on the toilet seat, I flip through Samuel's diary, looking for any clues that'll take me to Haley.

[October 16, 1948]

> *I wasn't going to ever write again. This*
> *book is full of bad memories, and so*
> *is Sevierville. Tennessee is just as I*
> *remember it: bleak, dusty—heavier*
> *than a goose-down comforter in sum-*
> *mertime. It feels a bit like purgatory.*
> *A lot of waitin. However, Nadia is*
> *here, and I never would have met her*
> *if I hadn't come back. We have a boy*
> *now: Henry. He's her spittin image. I*
> *never thought I'd be anyone's daddy.*
> *It just never seemed to be in the cards*
> *for a wretch like me. I sent photos to*
> *Wharton, and Rafe sent back photos of*
> *his little girl. Maybe we'll visit.*

Wharton. Where have I heard that name before? I
fish my phone out of my pocket, typing it into Google.
Wharton, Virginia, population: 4,753. I scroll through
aggregated photos, presumably taken by tourists,
#beachlife. Most are generic: a sun-reddened grin and
a swirly ice cream cone, a dog lazing on a beach towel,
and a seagull stealing a potato chip. A photo of the pier
draws my attention. There's a building with a clown's
face painted on the front, faded by the sun. Its grotesquely wide mouth frames the entrance. It's a funhouse. "The trip," I breathe, "that very last summer."

Flipping through Samuel's diary, there are other
references to Wharton, Virginia. There's a certain reverence for it, as though it's more than a seedy beach

town. It may as well be Mecca or Bethlehem. "'She's in Virginia,'" I murmur, repeating Cordelia's words. My voice echoes. I snap the book shut, stuffing it into the kangaroo pocket of my flannel pullover. It rests against my stomach, the sharp corner jabbing the sensitive spot just above my belly button. Before returning to the car, I stop in the atrium, slotting some loose change into the vending machine. I get two bottles of Coca-Cola, a bag of Fritos for myself, and a pack of Twizzlers for Cordy. They used to be her favorite.

When I get to the car, I glance around the lot. There's no one around except for a semi at the far end; his windows are covered with reflective sunshades and newspaper, so I expect the trucker is sleeping inside the cab. I unlock the trunk of my car, opening it wide. Cordelia flinches, raising her taped-together hands to cover her face. Despite the chill, she's sweating profusely, and the tape covering her mouth is curling at the corners. "Nnnn," she manages through the gag. She's sluggish and pliant—the ketamine worked like a charm. She was too sedated to transform, though that didn't stop me from glancing in the rearview mirror at every bump, expecting to see a furry fist punch through my trunk.

"I'm going to take the tape off, but you have to promise not to scream," I say. "Nod if you understand."

Cordelia nods, her blond hair sticking to her damp forehead. When I pinch the corner of the tape between my thumb and forefinger, her eyebrows furrow. "Mm-mmm!"

I rip it away. There's a smear of her lipstick on the sticky part of the tape. "What did you say?"

Cordelia presses her lips together. They are bright crimson, but I'm not sure if it's from the adhesive or her lipstick. She looks like a clown. "I said 'be gentle,'" she huffs. Clearly, I hadn't been.

I open the pack of Twizzlers, then place one of the licorice-flavored vines in her mouth. She chews it, sucking it into her mouth. Red saliva trickles out of the corners of her lips. "Sorry," I mutter because I am. I wish I had been brave enough to put her out of her misery. I had thought about it while she lay unconscious in the hall. If I rolled her onto her back, I wouldn't even have to look at her face while I did it. *It would be a kindness,* I wagered. Perhaps it would exorcize her demons, freeing her to ascend to those pearly gates. But just as with Samuel, I didn't have the stomach for it.

Swallowing, Cordelia awkwardly wipes her mouth with the side of her hand. "Why are you doing this?" she asks. I unscrew the cap of the Coke, the pneumatic *pshhht* inordinately loud in the quiet lot.

"I hope you like Coke," I say, pouring some of the fizzy liquid into her mouth. It dribbles messily down her chin, and I wipe her clean with my palm. She flinches as if I've struck her. Perhaps it's my hands— calloused and gritty like sandpaper.

"Because I need you to help me find her," I say, pulling a new strand of duct tape off the now-dwindling roll. "I need to find her before she kills again."

"Who?" Cordelia asks.

"Haley."

"My daughter? Why are you looking for my daughter?" She struggles to sit up, but only manages to prop herself up on one shaky elbow. I imagine most of her muscles are stiff and numb. She's been lying in the cramped trunk for hours now, the thin, rough-hewn liner doing little to protect her from the car's unforgiving aluminum frame.

"It's my divine mission," I reply. "She's rabid, you know."

Cordelia's brows knit together. "Haley would never hurt anyone."

Ah, to be a mother! Do they strap the blinders on just after the baby squelches out of the cervix? "The woman missing a leg at Knoxville General would disagree, I think." Without waiting for a rebuttal, I place the new strip of tape onto Cordelia's mouth. "We'll be in Wharton soon. Keep quiet, and maybe you'll survive."

I remember the Wharton Great Inn as being on par with the Ritz-Carlton. It's certainly upscale in the most performative sense. The plasterwork ceiling depicts dancing nymphs, though most of the figures appear to suffer from the pox; the plaster is dimpled and discolored by water and smoke. The man at the counter wears a three-piece suit, but it is lined with polyester and poorly tailored at the wrists. The complimentary coffee bar advertises hand-pulled espresso, but the only machine is a Keurig. A uniformed bellman pushes the cart laden with my—our—luggage and operates the elevator, but he has a tattoo of Marvin the Martian on his neck and earbuds in his ears.

As we ride to the fourth floor, I stare at Cordelia in the mirror. She's having trouble keeping her eyes open and slumps heavily against the wall. I think the second dose of ketamine was too high. Thankfully, the bellman is too engrossed in his music to notice. He hops from foot to foot, mouthing the words into the mirror.

The fourth floor smells faintly of stale cigarette smoke, though there are NO SMOKING placards posted every fifteen feet. Our room is midway down the hall, which isn't ideal. The bellman taps the keycard against the sensor, then pushes the cart inside to unload the bags. Cordelia sways beside me. "We're in a garden," she murmurs, staring down at the floral carpet.

"Shut up," I mutter out of the corner of my mouth.

The bellman returns, his cart empty. I hand him a five-dollar bill for the trouble. "Thank you, sir!" he chirps, stuffing the cash into the pocket of his slacks. They've been ironed so many times that the fold in the pleat is a shade lighter than the rest of the pants. "Enjoy your stay."

When the elevator car returns to collect the bellman and his cart, I herd Cordelia into the room and slide the deadbolt into place. "My mouth is so dry," Cordelia complains. "I need water."

The bathroom lights are inordinately bright, especially after the dim room. I pick the plastic wrap off of a glass cup, filling it from the tap. I once read that the cleaning service washes these glasses with the same sponge they use to scrub the toilet, but I don't think Cordelia will mind. She's miles away right now, circling a k-hole.

Cordelia has opened the curtains, and sunlight streams into the room. "Oh," she breathes, "we can see the beach. Look, Henry, the boardwalk! We've been here before, haven't we? It looks so familiar."

The Great Inn butts up against the pier, giving us a bird's eye view of the midway. A row of squat, clapboard booths house games of skill and chance. Tourists line up to toss balls at milk bottles hoping to win an oversized teddy bear or a dying goldfish imprisoned in a plastic bag. If I crane my neck just so, I can catch a glimpse of the funhouse, with its Pierrot-inspired facade. "We came when you were a toddler; I'm surprised you remember."

"Maybe I just remember the photos in the album," she muses, resting her cheek against the windowpane. "Isn't it funny how memory works?"

CHAPTER 9
(ANGUS)

———◁◆▷———

Blood is our commonality. Whether human or wolf, we can effectively be broken down into plasma, platelets, and cells. In the test tube and under the microscope, we are largely indistinguishable. I'm not entirely sure Hunter would be comforted by that fact, but I am.

The lab is empty—the hum of the centrifuge and the easy listening station my boss insists upon are my only companions. I've spent the last half-hour meticulously preparing blood smears, and when I finally get up from my station, the joints in my spine pop. I hadn't realized I was slouching, my shoulders butting up against my ears.

"You're a hard man to track down, Mr. Chilton." A man leans in the doorway. With his mule-colored woolen blazer and shiny Oxfords, he looks entirely out of place. Everyone in Wharton Med wears scrubs or johnnies, depending on which door you've come in.

"Am I?" I ask, pulling off my gloves. I reach for my coffee cup, taking a sip. It's cold. Perhaps he's a hospital administrator. They don't typically come down to the lab, preferring to stay cloistered in their ivory tower on the twelfth floor. "I didn't realize."

The man reaches into his blazer pocket, flashing a shield-shaped medallion. "Detective Acker, Wharton P.D." He smiles, his thin top lip disappearing beneath his bristly mustache.

"What can I do for you?" I dump what remains of my coffee in the trash before snapping on a fresh pair of gloves. I am careful to keep my voice even.

The detective prowls around the small, cold room, examining the autoclave, microscopes, and various analyzers. He taps the keyboard on the immunoassay analyzer, waking the machine.

"Don't touch that," I grumble. I know what he's doing. He may as well have lifted his leg and pissed on it.

"Well, let me amend that: you weren't hard for me to find. Your boyfriend was very forthright. You were, however, hard for Portland P.D to locate."

"I wasn't hiding. I moved. People do it all the time." I gather up my stack of slides, coasting on my wheeled chair to the microscope. The detective puts out his hand as if to stop my chair, but I breeze past him, unhindered.

"Surely you saw the news reports. Your boyfriend at the time, a mister…" He pulls out a small note-book, flipping through it. "…a Mr. James Volkov was a person of interest in a murder case."

I slot a slide into the microscope, peering into the viewfinder. The image is unfocused, and I crank the dial to adjust the lens. "I saw no reason to postpone my move because an ex got himself into trouble."

"An ex?" Acker stands right behind my chair, his hands on the desk; I'm effectively trapped. His hot breath wets my neck. His cologne is so strong it makes my eyes water. "It's strange you say that because when Portland was tracing James' steps the day before the Nedry murder, he was found on the security camera at Murata with you. You looked pretty cozy for 'ex's.'"

The neon sign in the window casts a bluish glow on James' skin. He surreptitiously plucks a piece of pork off of my plate with his chopsticks, dunking it into the tonkatsu sauce. When he slurps it into his mouth, his lips shine with grease. He licks them clean with his tongue.

"Hey! That's mine." I playfully kick his shin.

"I'm still hungry." Beneath the table, his fingertips walk up my knee.

"Order more sashimi," I snicker, popping a sliver of pork into my mouth. It's fatty and succulent, and I groan in delight. James' hand glides up my thigh. His pupils dilate, arousal quirking his brow. I find myself thinking of the tar pits that slurped the corpses of mammoths and saber-toothed cats into the earth, fossilizing them. If I look into his eyes too long, I will experience the same fate.

"Maybe I will," James replies. His lascivious sneer ignites a spark inside me. Embarrassed, I cast my eyes around the restaurant. None of the other diners seem to feel the electricity arcing between us, though their hair should be standing on end. James flags down a

waiter. *"Could I please get another order of sashimi—chef's choice?"*

As he orders, James brashly cups me through my jeans. His face is impassive, betraying nothing. I nearly jump out of my skin, rattling the table. My chopsticks clatter to the floor.

The waiter gives me a quizzical look. *"Can I get you anything else, sir?"*

"N-no, no! I'm great, thank you!" I duck beneath the tablecloth to retrieve my chopsticks, hoping the blush warming my cheeks will dissipate in the meantime. I surface to find James sipping his saké, looking like the cat who gobbled up the canary. He's in rare form tonight.

I toss my chopsticks onto the tablecloth. *"What's gotten into you?"*

James snags the last piece of pork off of my plate with his fingers, swirling it in the dark-colored sauce. He tips his head back to catch the dripping sauce in his mouth before it can stain the pristine tablecloth. *"The pork really is excellent,"* he remarks with the confidence of a gourmand.

"I can only imagine," I snort. *"You've eaten most of it."*

James' eyes sweep the dining room, finally settling on me. *"I read an interesting fact in a book today."* It's an odd segue—I'm not sure I've ever seen James darken the doorstep of a library, much less read a book.

"Oh?" I reach for the tokkuri, pouring a fingers' worth of saké into my cup. Taking a sip, I wince as the astringent taste adheres to the back of my tongue. I

chase it with ice water, but it only dilutes the bitterness
somewhat. My extremities tingle.

"Did you know that humans..." he leans for-
ward conspiratorially, whispering the word. "...taste
like pork?"

"I've heard that. 'Longpig,' they call it." I idly trace
the rim of my saké cup with my fingertip.

The waiter strides toward the table, carrying a
platter laden with sliced tuna, mackerel, and hamachi.
"Here you are, gentlemen," he says as he sets it in the
middle of the table. "The chef recommends dipping the
yellowtail in ponzu." He gestures toward the quartet of
ramekins from our last round of sashimi, housing soy,
ponzu, tamari, and wasabi dipping sauces. "Enjoy."

James wastes no time selecting a pink slice of
hamachi, dunking it into the watery Ponzu. This time,
it does drip on the tablecloth, and his shirtfront too.
But he doesn't seem to notice. He's talking with his
mouth full, flecks of fish jettisoning from his mouth
with every syllable. "Have you ever thought about
trying it?"

"I've had yellowtail before."

"No. Jesus, Gus. Pay attention. Have you ever
thought about eating humans?"

I chuckle, reaching for a fresh set of chopsticks. I
snap them apart like a wishbone, peeling off an errant
splinter. When I look up, James isn't laughing. He's
gripping his chopsticks in both hands, flexing the
flimsy wood. "I'm being serious. You've never thought
of it, even when wolfish?"

"Never," I scoff. It's unthinkable. He may as well
have asked if I thought about gargling the slime at the

bottom of the dumpster. "Have you?" I forget to hide the disgust in my voice and he flinches.

He jabs a wedge of raw tuna into the dollop of wasabi and then submerges it in the soy sauce. "Of course not. I'm not a monster."

"Maybe we did have dinner," I relent. "We had a messy breakup, and it was very on again-off again for weeks afterward. Our relationship was entirely dependent on his mood. I left without telling him I was going. He could be ... violent." I offer up partial truths, folding them inside pure fabrication.

The detective huffs but straightens. I can hear the rustling of his notebook and the scratch of a pencil, but I don't dare turn to look. I swipe at the microscope lens with a cloth.

"Interesting," Acker murmurs. "You'd think you'd feel some sort of civic duty to give the police that information after he was named a person of interest in a murder case."

"You keep saying that." I swivel in my chair, my elbows on the armrests in what I hope looks like nonchalance. "As if it means he did something."

Detective Acker cracks open the sharps container with his index finger, a low noise leaking from his throat. "I've always been scared of needles. Can you imagine? I took a vow to protect and serve—no matter the cost. But a blood draw turns me into a baby. I haven't gotten my cholesterol checked for damn near a decade."

I'm not entirely sure why he's taken this detour, but it feels like he's leading me toward a pitfall. "But," he continues, "you don't strike me as the avoidant type. The whole 'it's none of my business' shtick doesn't work for me."

"You've got me figured out, haven't you?"

"That's my job," he says. "Besides, I'm afraid I have an advantage. This is the first time we've met, but I've been digging into your life for weeks."

Gooseflesh crawls up my arms. I grit my teeth, tamping down my wolfish impulse to bash the detective's skull in with my chair. I imagine his blood pooling on the linoleum, staining the grout pink. "Is that why you were threatening Hunter?"

"Your Hunter sure is fragile if he thought that was a threat. It looked to me like we were having a cup of Joe."

I snicker, rolling across the aisle to open the lid of the centrifuge. I carefully lift out a PCR tray full of vials. "Hunter is a good judge of character."

"Oh yeah? What did he think of James?"

I place the PCR tray on the tabletop and the vials tremble in their slots, clinking together. "I told you: I left Portland alone."

Detective Acker clucks his tongue. He reaches inside his blazer, pulling out a piece of glossy paper. The edges are soft, one dog-eared. He's clearly been carrying it around for some time. With the glee of a card player revealing his winning hand, he places it before me. The monochrome photograph is grainy, a pixelated timestamp in the corner. It's a frame from a security camera's video feed. "This is from a Marathon Gas in Finley, Ohio."

Two cars occupy a small parking lot, the lights of the storefront illuminating their interiors. One is a sedan, with a driver and passenger inside. The other is a police cruiser, the driver's side door wide open. The officer leans against the hood of his vehicle, a cup of coffee in-hand. Detective Acker taps his finger on the sedan's driver; his nails are jagged and bitten to the quick. "That's you, isn't it?" He slides his finger over to the passenger. "'I left Portland alone.' That's what you said, right?"

"That's what I said," I croak around the lump in my throat. I grip the armrests. I can't explain away the figure as pareidolia. It's very clearly Luka, his hand splayed on the dash as he answered the officer's pointed questions ("West Coast, sir!"). Despite the pixelated image, I can even see the stripes on Luka's t-shirt, the curl pattern at his hairline.

"Interesting," the detective repeats. "I spoke with the officer in this photo. Baird, I think his name was. He said you were traveling with three passengers and a dog."

"He has a good memory," I mumble.

"You were memorable," Acker says, tucking the photo back into his pocket. "Apparently, Baird is into turkey hunting. He would not shut up about this Boykin Spaniel he hunts with. He said the dog in your car looked like it could take down a 'whole ass bear' — his words, not mine."

Sweat edges down the back of my neck. "I think I should call my lawyer."

"We're just having a conversation," Acker says, clapping his hand on my shoulder. The vein in my temple pulses in time with my heartbeat: fast and arrhythmic. "Y'know, it's funny, no one here in town has ever mentioned seeing you or Hunter walking a dog, but—"

I rise abruptly, the chair colliding with the detective's shins. "Look: I said I left Portland alone. I *did*. I made some friends on the way, and I offered them a ride. The dog belonged to one of them. I don't even remember their names now. I dropped one in D.C. and the other took a bus from Wharton to Tallahassee, I think."

Detective Acker's mustache twitches. "You didn't let me finish. I don't think the dog was a *dog* at all. I've lived in this town all of my life. My family has been in the police department for generations. I know what goes on here. I think you do too."

"I'm not sure what you're insinuating, but—"

A lanky man strides into the lab, a manila folder tucked under his arm and a box of donuts in hand. "How're those slides coming along?" Gary Welker asks. His Scottish burr, by way of county Durham, turns the words "how are" into a throaty purr. When he spots the detective, he pushes his thick glasses up his greasy, aquiline nose. "Oh! Can I help you?"

"I was just leaving," Detective Acker says, his eyes never straying from mine. "I just stopped by to give a friend some news."

Welker sets down his things at his workstation. "I hope it's good news," he says earnestly.

Detective Acker heads toward the door, buttoning his blazer over his belly. "Very good news. Isn't that right, Mr. Chilton?"

His cologne lingers for hours after he leaves.

CHAPTER 10
(HUNTER)

W hen it comes to scandal, Candace Bailey is like
a dog with a bone. She will gnaw at it until
her gums bleed, sticking her tongue into every nook
and cranny to taste the tender marrow. Today, I am
her quarry. "You were up late last night," she says,
bouncing on her toes. The wind whips down the alley,
scattering the refuse that didn't make the leap between
the dumpster and the garbage truck's hopper. She pulls
her thin cardigan more tightly around her shoulders.

I unlock the alley entrance to Ebb and Flow,
pushing the cinder block door stop into place with my
foot. The electricity has been turned off in the building,
and we'll need the daylight to see by. "I was watching
a movie," I comment, stepping carefully into the café's
scorched kitchen.

"You were staring out the window," Candy counters.
"Haley saw you when she went to get a cup of water."

I wish Candy wasn't here, but I had been driving us
both to work when I remembered what I had stashed
at the brick-and-mortar café. It felt reckless to leave

it there for another minute, let alone an entire shift—especially with the detective sniffing around like a bloodhound.

"It wasn't a good movie." A thick carpet of dust coats the floor. The pawprints of vermin traverse the room, skittering around the collapsed cabinetry. Gossamer tatting sags from the exposed rafters; the spiders have taken up residence in our absence. Somewhere in the building, I can hear a bird chirping. It must have gotten in through one of the blown-out windows before they were covered in plywood and, later, replaced. "We need to call an exterminator."

"We need to call a priest," Candy quips. She shines her iPhone's flashlight at the industrial fridge. Someone graffitied a sloppy pentagram on the brushed steel surface. The artist had an overzealous, unsteady hand. Rivulets of crimson paint run down to the floor, pooling like blood. I hurriedly avert my eyes. I've seen far too much blood spilled in my café.

"Some kids must have gotten in." I open the door to my office, finding it largely unscathed, save for a bit of soot around the doorjamb. Pulling open the bottom desk drawer, I thumb through the files therein. In the one labeled 34 Main Street, containing the building's deed and tax returns, I find the memory card. "Here it is," I breathe, relieved. I was afraid that I would come searching and it would be gone, pilfered by a certain interloping detective.

"What is that?" Candy asks.

"It's from the security camera out in the dining room before the first remodel. I never reinstalled it—thank god. It's from the morning that Angus was shot."

"Jesus, Hunt, why would you keep that? Have you been watching it? No wonder you don't sleep—"

I tuck the tiny SD card into my jean pocket, patting it through the fabric to make sure it's secure. "I never watched it. It just felt wrong to throw it away. Someone died."

The lie falls out of my mouth with ease; the truth is more rough-hewn, splintered with caveats. I watched it, but only once—only to see if the angle revealed the crime. I had almost forgotten what transpired after the dust settled.

Geoff is crying. He swipes at his leaking nose with the side of his hand, wiping the snot and blood onto his pants. "What the fuck is going on? What the fuck, Hunter?" His thin lips pull away from his teeth as he yowls.

Angus, his head cradled upon my crossed legs, hacks, a jettison of blood spewing from his mouth. "The ambulance is coming," I assure him. "I can hear the sirens." Gently, I finger-comb his tousled hair, tucking it behind his ears. My mother used to play with my hair when I was sick, massaging my scalp with her fingernails until it lulled me to sleep. Perhaps this small gesture will be a comfort to him too.

The empty gun sits on the floor beside me. Disgusted, I kick it away, and it skims across the linoleum until it collides with an overturned chair. Angus' breath rattles. If I laid my head on his chest, I imagine every inhale would sound like ice in a blender.

Geoff clambers to his feet, cradling his bitten forearm against his chest. The exertion makes him break into a sweat. Pale-faced, he shuffles toward the front door, but the fast-approaching sirens give him pause. Irresolute, he turns in a tight circle before shambling toward the double doors in the rear of the café. His vacant eyes sweep past me without a modicum of acknowledgment. He is on autopilot, his lizard brain steering him toward salvation.

"Where the fuck are you going?" I ask, resting my blood-slick hands on Angus' feverish skin. A fever means his body is fighting, right? Please fight, Angus!

"Away," Geoff manages. He inadvertently steps into the pool of Angus' blood, leaving scarlet shoe prints in his wake. "Away from here."

"What happened to 'none of us are leaving here alive,' huh?" The hypocrisy is staggering. But Geoff has always been a hypocrite.

Carefully, I rest Angus' head on the hard linoleum. I wish I had something to put under his head. His eyelids crinkle, but that's all. I imagine—I hope—he's somewhere far away from here. Perhaps, in his castle in the air, we are content, and there is no pain. I get to my feet, using a chair to heave myself up. My feet feel leaden and tingly. They've fallen asleep.

Despite my unsteadiness, I lunge at Geoff, grabbing fistfuls of his shirt in both hands. I am too forceful, and he stumbles against me, the back of his head colliding with my nose. I see stars. "You're going down for this!" I say as my left nostril whistles.

"Let go," Geoff pleads. The sirens are unmistakable now. They must be on the far end of Main Street, near the bus depot. They'll be here in a few minutes.

Geoff twists in my hands, stretching his t-shirt until the stitching at the shoulder pops. "Let go of me, Hunter!"

"You shot him!" As I scream, blood and spit freckles Geoff's face. "You don't get to just walk away."

Geoff palms my face with his functional hand, shoving me backward. I slip in Angus' blood and lose my grip on Geoff's shirt, falling onto my ass. "You're just as complicit here," Geoff says with a pointed jab of his finger at my face. "Remember that."

My anger boils over. My skin grows hot, my breath a ragged pant. "Fuck you," I snarl, barreling into him. We both tumble to the ground, nearly colliding with a café table. His head strikes the linoleum with a hollow thunk. *I find myself straddling his stomach, my hands splayed on his chest. His heartbeat is a staccato beneath my palm. The encroaching sunrise casts a pinkish glow over his startled face, making his skin appear waxy and corpse-like.*

I wish he was dead.

I punch him in the jaw, crying out when my knuckles split; thin blood seeps down the backs of my hands, four rivers branching off into tributaries at my wrist. I've never punched someone before. I've never been punched either. Geoff's fist drives my head sharply to the left, plucking every muscle in my neck like a guitar string. The gun is within arm's reach. It seems to emit a muted keening, like a scream underwater.

Or is that my ears ringing?

The metal is cold to the touch, heavy in my hand. When I look down at Geoff, all I see is gunmetal. He is just as frigid. He is just as burdensome.

*"What're you going to do with that?" Geoff spits.
"It's empty."
Grasping the weapon by the muzzle, I raise it over
my head. Geoff's eyes bulge in realization. Then, the
police breach the door, shouting at the both of us to
put our hands up.*

When I think about this moment later, I convince
myself I was only trying to frighten him. But the video
footage doesn't lie. Perhaps I'm not all that different
from the wolves, after all. However, they don't cry.
They don't lock themselves in a hospital bathroom
while their lover is in surgery, wiping blood off of
their hands with the brown paper towels that disinte-
grate when moist. They don't heave into the toilet nor
hyperventilate.

"Hunter? Are you okay?" Candy waves her hand in
front of my face. *Earth to Hunter.*

"Yeah, sure. Let's get out of here." I brush past her,
but she grips my wrist.

"You know, I'm really worried about you. We really
haven't talked about what happened here, the outburst
at Thanksgiving, Angus moving out. I—"

I shake her off. "Candace, last time you were
'really worried,' you were ready to check me into the
psych ward. Pardon me for not wanting to discuss any
of this with you." I'm being cruel; I know that.

Candy flinches. "Hunter, that was well over a year
ago. I apologized—profusely. I didn't have all the
information—"

"Yeah, you never do."

"What's that supposed to mean?" She threads the strap of her purse through her fingers, biting at her lower lip. It makes her look like a child.

"You talk a lot for someone so willfully ignorant."

"Well, you're mean and paranoid," Candy counters, tears welling in her eyes. "That's why you've been staying up all night, isn't it? You're keeping watch. And for whom? No one is coming for you."

"'No one is—!?'" I sputter. "I killed someone! I have a detective's business card burning a hole in my pocket." I head toward the back door, suddenly desperate to get out of the stuffy café and Candy's crosshairs. I brush against the wall, a tuft of exposed fiberglass insulation clinging to my shoulder. Gingerly, I tug the batting off of my sweater with my thumb and forefinger, tossing it aside. The smell of burnt adhesive lingers on my skin even after I wipe my hands on my jeans. It is poetic that the café's innards are pink, malodorous, and dangerous to touch.

"He doesn't know anything about you. Angus can handle everything else," Candy insists. She is so close that she nearly steps on my heels. I burst from the building, gulping in the crisp wintry air. "Can't you see that you're dismantling your entire life, brick by brick?" she continues.

I want to clap my hands over my ears to drown her out, but that would be infantile. I may as well stick my tongue out at her. "Angus can't protect anyone. Look at how many people have died in just eighteen months!"

Candy sighs, running her fingers through her hair. "Have you ever thought that you're making it worse?

It's like you scraped your knee and decided to spit in it rather than get a band-aid."

There is nothing more to say. She's put my secret fear into words. I fish my keys out of my pocket. "Just get in the car. We're late."

I toss the SD card into the blender, pouring in a cupful of water for good measure. It blends beautifully, tiny shards of plastic and circuitry swirling amidst the blades. The coffee sifter makes an adequate strainer. I pick out the remains of the card, careful to get every scrap. Then I toss the pieces in the dumpster behind the bus. The ritual should be a relief, but I find myself worrying that even my due diligence won't be enough.

Candy isn't speaking to me. She sits on the stool at the service window, twisting her hair around her fingers. She twists it around and around until the strand eventually snaps, the shedding hair floating around the cab until it is eventually sucked into the vent at her feet. I want to tell her that's unsanitary, but it'll only encourage her to continue pestering me.

I find myself thinking of Angus. *Angus can't protect anyone,* I'd said. But that's not true. He is capable and strong, but he is spread far too thin. The others have tools to protect themselves—teeth, claws, and an accelerated immune system—but I may as well be made of paper. One misstep and I'm dead. He could give me those implements if he wanted, but he likes me soft and small.

"Are you open?" An older gentleman in a Wharton Beach crewneck sweatshirt sidles up to the counter, rapping his knuckles on the metal. A woman stands beside him, her hands deep in the pockets of her ivory puffer jacket. While we are smack dab in the middle of the off-season, they are clearly tourists. Tourists are easy to spot: they smile just a smidge too widely. They ask inane questions, even when the answer is written on the chalkboard just inches from their face. They wear merch featuring their vacation destination.

"Yep," I say, "what can I get you?"

The man glances at his companion. She stares dreamily at the chalkboard menu, her lips moving wordlessly. "Two black coffees," he finally decides. I pour from the still-warm carafe, slipping the cups into cardboard sleeves stamped with the Ebb and Flow logo.

"Are you enjoying Wharton?" I ask as I pop on the lids.

"It's changed a lot," the man says. "We visited as kids back in the mid-60s." When he says 'we' he gestures to his companion. On second glance, the man and woman look somewhat similar: they have the same ski-slope nose and ash tone in their hair. However, the woman's hair is blond while the man's skews gray. Perhaps they are siblings or one of those couples who morph into a single organism after years of cohabitation. I think of the phenomena whenever I inadvertently put on a pair of Angus' socks instead of my own. Or rather, I did. Before he left and took his socks with him.

While the man pays, the woman wanders to the other end of the long counter. "Do you happen to have any Splenda?" she asks my sister. Her voice is timid.

"Sure," Candy says, sliding off of her stool. She stands on tiptoes to reach into the overhead cabinet, pulling down the bulk box of Splenda. Setting it on the counter, Candy pulls out an individual packet. "Sorry it's not out on the table with the rest of the mix-ins. No one ever asks for Splenda anymore," she says by way of apology. "Something about the sucralose."

The woman accepts the sachet of faux sugar as though it is a treasured gift. Suddenly, she grasps Candy's wrist, nearly tugging her over the counter. "Your perfume!" she exclaims. "What scent is it?"

Candy jerks her hand back. "I'm not wearing any," she answers. To her credit, her customer service facade does not waver. An overzealous customer hardly registers on the impropriety scale. Once, an irate customer threw a cheese danish at her head because she'd forgotten to warm it up for him. While I count out the older man's change, I keep an eye on the situation.

"It's so familiar," the woman remarks, seemingly unaware of her faux pas. "It's like summertime, that smell right when the sprinkler turns on."

"I guess I just naturally smell nice," Candy chuckles humorlessly.

"It reminds me of my d—" The woman's comment is cut off by her companion, who coughs loudly. When his fit subsides, he ignores my outstretched hand and the $1.75 in my palm. He coolly picks up the coffees.

"Keep the change," he says. "Let's *go*, Cordelia."

113

CHAPTER 11
(ANGUS)

————◁◆▷————

In wintertime, twelve-hour shifts can be brutal. I walk into the hospital before dawn and leave well after dusk. The lab has no windows, so the only time I see daylight is when I venture up to the cafeteria for a lukewarm slice of pizza or a wilting salad. Most of my cohorts work every other shift to get a brief reprieve. I find the tedium comforting. It's as though I'm in stasis—asleep in some pod light-years from here, suspended in goo.

At work, I don't think about Hunter Bailey. It's only when I walk to my car, my lab coat draped over my arm, that he materializes at my side. I rehash arguments during my commute, searching for the precise moment when it all went wrong.

While Hunter once looked at me with yearning in his eyes, now there is disdain. At first, I mistook it for ennui. Surely, the novelty wore off—with time, the unimaginable can become unremarkable. Even a werewolf forgets to put the toilet seat down or inadvertently leaves the damp clothes to mold in the washer. But we didn't slip into the easy intimacy of longtime partners either. Instead, we ping-ponged from one waking nightmare to another. Perhaps we weren't in a relationship at all, but instead, we were trauma-bonded.

There were moments when I got Hunter back: a joke told; place settings for two at the kitchen table; his hand beneath my waistband, his skin feverish with want. These moments gave me hope, which he would extinguish with gusto. It's almost as though he took some perverse joy in snuffing it out, sucking the oxygen from the room. *If I'm suffocating, you're suffocating too.*

When I turn onto Bird's Nest, the crunch of gravel brings me back to the present. My headlights sweep over the bungalow that Hunter and I shared. The curtains are open, and I catch a glimpse inside the dark living room as I drive past. The television is on, the screen painting a swath of crimson across Hunter's face. He's asleep, his chin tucked into his chest and his mouth slack. My knuckles blanch on the wheel, wanting desperately to pull into the driveway.

I imagine unlocking the door and slipping inside, waking Hunter with a kiss on the forehead. "Let me tuck you into bed," I'd say, urging him to his feet. "We don't have to talk—not tonight." In my fantasy, he lets me lead him to the bed we once shared with its white sheets and decorative pillows. His eyelids droop as I unbutton his jeans and shuck his t-shirt up over his head. The static makes his hair stand on end, and we laugh as I smooth it against his scalp. When I tuck him into bed, he reaches for my wrist, urging me to stay.

Instead, I continue onward. I pass the dunes, carpeted in wispy sea grass. I think that I see a dark-colored wolf standing very near the remnants of the fateful bonfire, but when I tap the brake and crane my neck for a second look, it is gone. Surely, it was a figment of my imagination. I haven't been sleeping well on Ama's fold-out couch. The springs pinch my skin every time I so much as roll over, and it is never quiet. The house groans and creaks, and the dryer seems to always be in the middle of a cycle.

Beyond the dunes, the ocean slow-rolls, the water nearly indistinguishable from the cloudless sky. I catch a glimpse of Renner's boat, moored just offshore. The anchor light bobs, illuminating the barnacle-laden hull and the white-capped waves slapping against the fiberglass. I can't bear to sell it, so the boat deteriorates in the slip I've rented for it. Renner's ashes are onboard, strapped to his captain's chair with a bottle of Johnnie Walker alongside. Sometimes, I climb aboard to sit beside his chair, telling my friend about the goings-on he's missed in the weeks since his passing.

The lights blaze in Ama's bungalow and my nerves twang. Something isn't right. Ama Chilton is parsimonious to a fault, and she would never leave them on. "We don't need to light the whole neighborhood" is a common refrain in her home. Even the Christmas lights get turned off before she goes to bed.

Before I can take off my seatbelt, the door swings open. Ama and Toby stumble out, the pregnant teen leaning heavily on my grandmother's shoulder. In the porch light, Toby's olive skin appears pallid, sweat beading on her brow. They are able to shuffle to the steps before Toby stops in her tracks, letting out a strangled scream. She reaches for the stair rail, gripping it so hard I fear splinters will embed in her palms. "Start the car, Aggie," Ama calls. "We've got to go to the hospital."

While Ama's voice is even, there's an edge to it. The baby isn't due for another month.

When the contraction passes, Ama ushers a breathless Toby down the stairs. Whimpering, Toby climbs into the back of my car, not bothering to smooth the wrinkles in her tiered skirt. Ama carefully pulls the seatbelt over her lap, clicking it into place. "Safety first," Ama adds cheerfully.

I meet Toby's eyes in the rearview mirror as Ama ambles around the car. "It's too early," Toby sniffles. "This can't be happening—not now."

"It'll be alright," I assure her. "That baby is made of strong stuff, and so are you." I didn't intend to sound hackneyed and corny, but judging by Toby's frown, I've been less than reassuring.

As soon as Ama gets into the front seat, I throw the car into reverse, the tires kicking up gravel. I drive fast, jerking the wheel to pass slower vehicles on the narrow road. In the back, Toby howls, curling around her cramping belly. "Breathe," Ama reminds her. While my grandmother sounds outwardly composed, she grips the armrests with both hands.

As I turn onto Carson Avenue, Toby's fist slams into the back of my chair. In the rearview mirror, her face contorts. Her jaw snaps, her crowded teeth jutting above her upper lip in an exaggerated overbite. She chokes on her swelling tongue, her face bright red. "Toby!" I shout. "You can't do this right now!"

Toby can't answer. The contractions come one on top of another, the breaking of her bones turning her into a fount of pain. She fumbles with her seatbelt, freeing herself from the restraint to labor on hands and knees across my backseat. Her spine juts through her soaking wet tank top, the vertebrae rolling like a wave beneath her skin.

"You need to pull over, Aggie," Ama says. "She's not going to make it to the hospital, and she can't show up like this."

The chimera in the backseat bangs her head against the window. "Help," she manages around her tongue. "Can't … stop it."

"Pull over?" I laugh. This close to Christmas, the sidewalk is crowded with pedestrians. I imagine parallel parking in front of Seaside Books, delivering a baby while Ama serenely slots quarters into the meter.

Fluid splatters on the leather seat, and I wince. "Oh!" Toby exclaims. "Water … broke."

"The alley behind the café," Ama insists, grasping my forearm. "Angus, *now!*" She glances back at Toby, writhing in a puddle of amniotic fluid.

"Fuck *me*." I cut the wheel, the front tire mounting the curb. Speeding down the alley, I inadvertently sideswipe a dumpster. My sideview mirror flies off, leaving behind only a knot of wire. The café is midway down the alley that runs parallel to Main Street, stretching from Main to Jefferson. While the rear of the café— with its fire escape and allotted dumpster—is identical to its neighbors, I find it with no trouble. The corner of the dumpster is crumpled as if struck by an enormous fist.

"This isn't the hospital," Toby cries. A fat tear trickles down her cheek, dampening the fur sprouting there. "Please, Angus, keep driving."

Wordlessly, I climb out of the idling sedan. The alleyway is narrow, not unlike the cow chute on a killing floor. With the driver's side door yawning open, the car blocks the bidirectional lane. We should be undisturbed. Pedestrians prefer the well-lit sidewalks, and the only vehicle that takes this particular route is the municipal garbage truck. I open Toby's door, kneeling so that I can look her in the eye.

Toby whines, her long tongue dangling from her mouth. With her lower jaw jutting out and her nose upturned, she resembles a brachycephalic dog. She sounds like one too—every exhale is accompanied by a wheeze. "Listen to me, Toby. You're not going to make it to the hospital. You're in too much pain, and the wolf is trying to help you. We already have more than enough humans who know about us."

"No," Toby growls. "I was promised an epidural, ice chips—I'm not doing this in a fucking alley." A contraction ripples through her, and she slumps against the back of the passenger seat. She burps up a bit of foamy bile, swiping at her mouth with the back of her hand. "I'm not doing this here."

"We're going up to the loft," I assure her. "Now c'mon, before the next contraction."

Ama produces an embroidered handkerchief from her purse, turning in her seat to dab at Toby's lips. "Did you know I gave birth to Angus' mama in my bathtub?

I promise you, child, your body knows what to do. The wolf will help you. Angus will make sure you have somewhere comfortable and safe to do this." Ama glances at me, jerking her chin toward the building. *Go.*

It's not difficult to break into the loft. I am tall enough on tiptoes to grab the lowest rung of the fire escape. The metal squeals and spits rust, but with a firm tug, the ladder comes down. I climb up to the second story and find new windows, with the manufacturer's sticker still plastered on the frames. Fortunately, whoever installed them didn't bother to lock them afterward. There's nothing inside worth stealing.

Inside, the air is stagnant and soupy. It reeks as though an animal sought refuge inside the refrigerator and died, but I suspect it's rotting food. The walls — once white, I think — are dappled with soot. I imagine if I touch them, they'll leave a greasy, smelly residue on my fingertips. The detritus of Candace Bailey's life remains in the garret, including furniture, clothing, and a crusty bowl in the sink. I think that it might have once contained oatmeal.

I unlock the front door and hurry downstairs to let Ama and Toby into the building. Toby leans against the dumpster. When I lift her into my arms, she is clammy to the touch. "I can't do this," she mumbles as I carry her up the stairs and into the muggy loft. "He's going to die. It's too early."

Gently, I lay her in Candy's bed. The sheets are dusty but otherwise clean. Almost immediately, a contraction ratchets her in half, and wheat-colored fur ripples down her back. The strap of her tank top rips at the seam. Toby curls up on her side, burying her face in one of the overstuffed pillows. It does very little to muffle her screams or the crackle of bone. She reaches for my hand, squeezing my fingers tightly. Her palm is calloused. What was once skin is now a thick layer of adipose and fiber: the emergence of paw pads.

Ama hustles around the loft. She finds clean towels in the bathroom and an unopened bottle of Dasani in the foul-smelling refrigerator. She hums as she works, pouring the water into the kettle still perched on the stovetop. The gas burner lights with the help of a match, though it fills the loft with the acrid smell of rotting eggs. She piles the towels on the foot of the bed, giving Toby's leg a gentle squeeze. "Let's get your tights off, sweetheart," Ama croons. "Angus, go check on my water."

Gently, I disentangle my hand from Toby's iron-clad grip. I edge around the privacy screen with its cherry blossom motif, grateful for the excuse to leave, if only momentarily. I'm out of my depth here. While the water in the kettle rolls, it's not quite boiling. I lean against the counter beside the stove to wait.

"Oh, it hurts!" Toby groans from behind the screen. "There's so much pressure!" Her voice is gravelly now.

"The baby is coming, Toby," Ama assures her. "Listen to me: with the next contraction, you are going to push. Push as hard as you can, curl into it. Angus, forget the water. I need you to hold her leg!"

I rush back over to Toby's bedside. The creature in the bed isn't Toby anymore. The sandy-colored wolf grips the bedsheets, her dark lips pulled away from her pale gums. My grandmother sits at the foot of the bed, dwarfed by the wolf's muscular thighs. Ama doesn't acknowledge me, her hands working between Toby's legs. "He's breech," she says, "I can feel his foot. He's too far down to turn him."

"I can't, I can't!" Toby rises onto all four paws atop the bed, her tail twitching in agitation. Her limbs tangle amidst the bedspread, but she doesn't seem to notice. Her spine bows, fighting against the imminent contraction. "It's not safe. He's too little," she sobs. With wolfish lips and teeth, the sobs sound not unlike phlegmy coughs.

When I reach out to touch Toby's shoulder, the muscle twitches beneath my palm. "He's got a whole family to come meet," I remind her.

Toby swings her head in my direction, her snout wrinkled. "No!" The growl rumbles like thunder. "Hunter's right: they've all died."

Ama, undeterred, lifts the wolf's tail. "I can see both feet and a loop of the umbilical cord. It could be wrapped around his neck; we need to do this now!"

"No!" Toby whirls, her teeth snapping inches from Ama's head. "At least ... at least if he's inside me, he never has to be scared. He never has to be scared like Renner was."

I can't help but think of Renner's sightless eyes, looking up at the sunrise. *I've got you, buddy,* I said, my eyes on the knife blade lodged between his vertebrae. With his every rattling breath, I imagined the keen edge severing the spinal cord. "I'm not going to let anything happen to you," I assure her. "I promise."

Ama meets my eyes over the wolf's trembling flank. "You know you can't promise her that, Aggie."

"A-Ama," I stammer, uncomprehending. Surely, she wants Toby to be more pliant, to focus. What good is arguing with me?

"You can't know what will happen tonight. You are an Alpha, but you aren't infallible. It's a title that's been bestowed on you because you are a leader, nothing more. Perhaps you're naturally gifted—you are a Chilton, after all—but you aren't more than the sum of your pack." When another contraction swells, Ama drives her palms into Toby's hips. "Does the counterpressure help?" she asks her patient.

Toby doesn't answer, gnashing her teeth. A flurry of goose down rains down upon our heads as she digs her claws into a pillow. An errant feather lands upon the tip of my nose, and I swipe it off, agitated. "This isn't the time for a lecture, Granny!" I snap.

Screeee, the kettle trills.

"What you can promise her is that you'll be beside her until the bitter end. *That's* who an Alpha is, Aggie: someone who sees the strength in others and harnesses it. This impulse of yours to fall on every sword isn't working," Ama continues, undeterred.

I whirl, intending to go take the kettle off the burner, but Toby grasps my forearm. "Please don't leave me," she murmurs. I sink down onto the mattress beside her, pulling her enormous head into my lap.

"Never," I promise, knowing it's one I can keep. "Now, when Granny says 'push,' you push!"

CHAPTER 12
(HUNTER)

---◁◆▷---

The chairs in the waiting room are straight-backed and unforgiving. Every time I lean forward and then back again, the vinyl upholstery sticks to the strip of exposed flesh between my shirt hem and waistband. I tug at my flannel button-down for the umpteenth time, grumbling curses under my breath. Candy, sitting in the row opposite, raises her eyebrows. She's still wearing the overly large t-shirt she wore to bed, half-tucked into a pair of sweatpants I think she might have pilfered from my closet. Her hair is a snarl atop her head.

At least this waiting room is more cheerful than the one attached to the surgical unit. That room had been windowless, dim, and depressingly beige. The television was far too loud, without any means of lowering the volume. Any nurse I begged to save me from the scripted banter on QVC simply shrugged and said, "The remote is around here somewhere." It's as though they thought noise would subdue our anxieties.

Instead, it made me want to pull my hair out, strand by strand.

Comparatively, the labor and delivery waiting room is sunlit with floor-to-ceiling windows on the far wall. The walls are a calming blue, framed photos of airbrushed babies adorning every wall. The television is muted and colorful cartoon animals frolic across the screen. The windows offer a view of would-be parents crossing the pedestrian bridge from the parking garage across the street, carrying unwieldy car seats and suitcases chock full of their hopes and dreams. Everyone is overly friendly. A man waiting at the vending machine shows me a sonogram of his granddaughter. "She's going to call me pop-pop!" he says excitedly.

Haley, pacing the aisle, pulls her phone out of the back pocket of her overalls. She stares at the screen. "Anything from Angus?" I ask. I know I sound wounded. He'd texted his packmate, not me.

"Not since the text three hours ago," she replies. "'Wharton Med. L&D. Baby is here.'"

"I'm going to get another coffee." It'll be my third trip to the vending machine. We've been here since 4:30 a.m., waiting for a crumb of information. The nurses, though polite, hadn't been particularly forthcoming because we aren't Toby's family. My back protests when I pop up out of my chair, and I stretch, bending over to touch my toes. When I straighten up again, Angus is standing in the doorway. He looks exhausted, the skin under his eyes dark and puffy. He's wearing his scrubs, and tiny, white feathers cling to his shoulders, though he doesn't seem to notice.

"Asher Sebastian Young, four pounds even," he announces, adjusting his eyepatch. "He's named after Toby's great-grandfather and some actor she likes. He's in the NICU, but he's going to be okay."

Angus sinks into the chair beside Candy, his elbows on the armrests. Our eyes meet across the aisle, and my breath hitches. It's the first time I've seen him since I warned him about the detective.

"How's Toby?" Candy asks. She's chewing gum, her jaw working like a cow munching on its cud.

"Tired," he answers, rubbing at his eyes with the heels of his hands. "She got to hold him in the ambulance but hasn't gotten cleared to go to the NICU to see him. They are giving her an EEG. Her heart rate was very fast when we arrived."

"He was born at the house?" Haley asks.

"Not quite," Angus admits. He glances around the room, making sure we won't be overheard. The expectant grandfather sits on the other end of the room, reading a battered issue of Elle. "IT'S SUMMER— TIME TO SLAY!" the cover declares.

"We were on our way here, but the baby was coming, and Toby couldn't ... control herself. We ended up breaking into Ebb and Flow and stayed there 'til the baby was born." He smiles apologetically at my sister. "I owe you a new mattress."

"Toby must have been so frightened," Haley says, nibbling at her cuticles.

"She did beautifully. Ama delivered the baby, but he was listless. He came out feet-first and was blue. I breathed into him, and he perked up pretty quickly. He was trying to latch when the ambulance showed up."

"Wow," I murmur.

Angus shoots me a strange look but doesn't comment. Instead, he rises, adjusting the nametag dangling from his pocket. In the ID photo, he is smiling, his long hair tucked behind his ears like a schoolboy. "I heard something about coffee. Where can I find some?"

"Down the hall," Candy answers, jerking her thumb over her shoulder. "There's an alcove just past the nurse's station. It tastes like shit."

Angus lingers for a moment, shifting from foot to foot. He stuffs his hands into the pockets of his scrub pants. The motion tugs down the waistband just a hair, revealing a sliver of pale flesh and a thatch of dark hair. "Hunter, can I talk to you for a minute?" he asks softly.

I nod, wordlessly, trailing him down the hall. In the alcove, we stand side-by-side, staring at the trio of vending machines. Angus pats at his pockets. "Shit," he murmurs. "Do you have a dollar?"

"Yeah, I think so." I fish out my wallet, producing a bill. Angus accepts it with a grateful quirk of his lip. Feeding the bill into the slot, he selects a black coffee, watching the dark liquid *drip, drip, drip* into a Styrofoam cup.

"How are you?" Angus asks.

"Fi—" The word is nearly out of my mouth before I think better of it. What good will it do to lie? We've never lied to each other before, no matter how ugly the truth was. "I don't know," I admit.

"Same." Angus' hands are back in his pockets now. He bounces on his toes, clicking his tongue. "I just wanted—needed—to tell you that I'm sorry. I have been so caught up in *being* an Alpha, that I haven't been *acting* like one. I've been making promises I can't keep."

"Oh?"

"It felt like the easiest thing to promise someone: 'I'll keep you safe.' But, in trying to do that, I took away your agency. I stopped listening. And I failed because of that. You lost everything, and I'm sorry." His big body trembles.

I feel a little off-kilter. I never thought that Angus would admit he was wrong. I had started to believe that maybe, in all actuality, I had been. After all, I had spoken in anger. I was filled with white-hot malice that made me vicious and spiteful. The anger boiled in my belly until it became as hard as obsidian. I had imagined that the only way to relieve the ache of it was to crush it into little pieces, expelling it like a kidney stone. But Angus? He was calm and resolute. He spoke without spitting, his words carefully chosen and laid out like a poker hand. It is easy to feel wrong when your opponent is wearing mirrored sunglasses and all you see is your own bulging eyes.

Tentatively, I touch his arm. The muscle flexes beneath my fingertips. "Thank you for saying that."

The last of the coffee sputters out of the tap, missing the cup entirely. Angus doesn't reach for it. "I love you, Hunter," he admits, finally turning to look at me. "I know that we have a lot to talk about—to work through. But I couldn't go another day without saying that."

"I love you too," I whisper. We are so close that our breath comingles. There are wiry gray hairs intermixed in his scruffy beard. I've never noticed them before.

Though, it's been quite some time since we've been this close.

Angus' breath quickens, his eyes darting around the alcove. While it's somewhat secluded, nurses walk the hallway at regular intervals. Someone will absolutely come in here for the same reason we had; the siren song of cheap coffee is inordinately loud, especially in a unit where the plaintive wails of newborns leak through the vents. "Come on," Angus urges, grasping my hand.

He leads me to a nondescript door just down the hall. I catch only a brief glimpse of a mop and bucket before Angus shuts the door behind us. It is pitch dark in the closet, and I bump into something that clatters noisily to the floor. Angus shushes me.

"Where are—?" The smell of bleach burns my nostrils.

Angus' mouth crushes mine, his tongue spilling between my teeth as though he plans to devour me from the inside out. The brash familiarity of his touch makes me whimper. He steps over the yawning chasm between us as though it's but a crack in the sidewalk. There is desperation in his touch, and a growl leaks from between his gritted teeth. He's always been careful to conceal his wolfishness in bed, not wanting to frighten me. But right now, the wolf wants me too.

"What if someone comes?" I mumble into his mouth. My hands alight on his chest, holding him at bay. His pectoral muscles jump; he is a racehorse crashing against the starting gate, desperate to run. His scrub top is pilling and worn thin from regular washing, and I can feel the *thump-buh-thump* of his heart against my palm. Perhaps that's why I haven't been able to sleep. I was so used to resting my head on his chest, listening to the metronome of him. Without it, I heard everything else: the wheeze of the air conditioner, the creak of the foundation, the branches scratching against the window, the slow roll of the ocean when the tide was high.

"Janitorial staff won't clock in 'til nine o'clock," Angus assures me. He sucks my lower lip between his teeth, making me hiss; pain and pleasure spark like twin flames. Heat pools in my core. I desperately missed his touch. He guides me back against the wall, and something digs painfully into the small of my back. It's a dustbin, hanging on a nail.

Angus pushes my flannel shirt off my shoulders. The sudden chill makes my areolas pucker. His insistent lips trail down my neck, his teeth grazing against my clavicle. When he falls to his knees at my feet, an ecstatic shiver overtakes me. The anticipation of his touch is torturous. He nuzzles my soft belly just above my waistband. "I missed you," he murmurs.

"I missed you too," I pant. I've only had my dreams to sustain me, waking to damp sheets and hazy memories that fade before I turn on the bedside lamp. Angus tugs my jeans down to my knees. My erect cock strains against the silken fabric of my boxer briefs. If he so much as breathes on me, I swear that I'll cum.

He peels down my underwear and gooseflesh prickles on my thighs. I reach for anything to bolster me, the back of my hand striking a shelving unit. I thread my fingers through the wire mesh. In the dark, I can only see his silhouette—a void amidst shadows.

My eyes play tricks on me: pointing his ears, adding bulk to his already broad frame. Something swishes, and I am not sure whether it's the shuffle of his knees on the linoleum or a wagging tail.

Suddenly, his hot mouth envelops me, his tongue pressing against the sensitive spot just beneath the swollen glans. "Angus!" I groan, fisting his hair with my free hand. He cups my ass, his nails dimpling the flesh. I buck my hips wantonly. The head of my cock butts up against his soft palate, and my balls clench.

"I'm—" I manage before an orgasm quakes through me. Before I can catch my breath, Angus' mouth is on mine. I can taste the brine of my skin and semen on his tongue.

"Turn around," he commands. With my jeans around my knees, I have to take short, mincing steps. Angus loses patience, grasping my shoulder and shoving me against the wall. I gasp. "Sorry," he murmurs. "Are you okay?"

"Yeah."

"I ... need to fuck you. Now." He spits into his palm. He hasn't been this prurient in a long time. It reminds me of the first time we ever touched, when he made me cup his thickening cock through his pants. *What do you want, Hunter?*

My cheek resting upon the drywall, I listen to him pant as he strokes himself. He stands so close that his knuckles butt up against my hip. There's a rawness to him that I haven't experienced since our very first encounter. He quakes as though fighting himself, every subsequent touch a test of his own humanity. I wonder if he ever stops thinking about breaking me.

His cock nestles between my cheeks, but he doesn't push past the tight ring of muscle. Not yet. Instead, he licks my neck, burying his nose in my hair. Then he presses inside me, the bulbous head of his cock stretching me well past comfort. He is gentle as he slides into my heat, muttering platitudes into my ear. After a few gentle thrusts, his speed quickens, his hips crashing into me. Every ragged exhale is a puff of wet heat on my skin. Before he cums, he wraps his hand around my neck, tipping my head back so that he can kiss my mouth. "Mine," he growls, as though I could ever forget.

CHAPTER 13
(HENRY)

——◁◆▷——

Sevierville, Tennessee—August 1970

After the cool, dim movie theater, the summer sun sears my eyes. The air appears to shimmer just above the blistering sidewalk. I imagine that, if it were to become even one degree hotter, the shimmer would morph into a full-fledged mirage. If I were to see one, I imagine I would see an ice cream truck, piloted by a grinning Good Humor man doffing an officer's cap. Dripping drumsticks and creamsicles would float around it like satellites. I regret the fistfuls of popcorn I ate during the film; the salt sucked all of the moisture from my mouth.

"What did you think of the movie?" My mother's blocky heels clack on the sidewalk. They always make me think of horses' hooves. I cast a sidelong look at the row of movie posters adorning the wall, the words NOW PLAYING emblazoned above each. I'd wanted to see *Bonnie and Clyde*, but mom insisted we see the latest Dominic Valentine picture, *Virtues and Valentines*. The poster for *Bonnie and Clyde* promised a car chase and a shootout, while *Virtues and Valentines* only promises a lingering stare that culminates in a kiss. Barf.

"What did *you* think?" I counter. I don't want to be a bummer.

"I think that I had a wonderful afternoon with my marvelous son," she says, smiling down her ski-slope nose at me. She's still holding the popcorn bag, and she pops one of the few remaining kernels in her mouth. "Dominic Valentine was very handsome, too."

"Mom!" I wrinkle my nose and stick out my tongue. "That's gross."

She laughs, playfully elbowing me in the ribs. "When you're older, you'll appreciate a love story."

"Yeah, when I'm five hundred, like you!" I say teasingly. The parking lot—the asphalt baking—seems to stretch on forever. By the time we reach the pickup, my shirt sticks to my back. It is hotter inside the cab, and I have to use my shirttail to grab my seatbelt.

"Samuel must be sweltering," my mother says as she starts the engine. Hot air coughs out of the air conditioning vent. Sam is with the veterinarian today, gelding my colt, Alban. That's why I got to go to the movies—mom wanted to spare me the sight of it.

When we get onto the highway, I roll down my window. The humid air musses my hair, slapping at my cheeks. "Roll that up," my mother urges. "You're letting the cool air out."

I want to say, *What gosh darn 'cold air'?* Instead, I roll the window up. Now that I'm about to start eighth grade, I've been thinking a lot about swear words. Perhaps that's because I'm nearly an adult, and swears roll off adults' tongues like spittle. If I were so bold as to utter them aloud, instead of practicing them in my head, mama'd make me sit in the bathroom with a bar of soap between my jaws 'til I farted bubbles.

The heat is putting me in a foul mood. It disgusts me that she talks about my stepfather with the same breathless yearning as Dominic Valentine. She sighs his name: S-*ahhh*-muel. I always thought my mother was a good person—a good judge of character. She's the sort of mom a kid would look to for help when they skinned their knee on the playground. She can't pass a mite-ridden puppy in a cardboard box outside Winn-Dixie without scooping it up. That's how we got two of the three farm dogs. But are you truly good if you surround yourself with hellfire—if you lay down beside the Beast every night? "Do you ever miss dad?" I ask. "Being married to him, I mean."

My mother drives with one hand on the wheel, the other on the knob of the gear stick. The hand on the stick spasms, and she nearly throws the truck into neutral. The truck balks, slowing just a smidge. The Plymouth riding our bumper honks. My mother waves out the window, mouthing *sorry* in the rearview mirror, though there's no way the driver could possibly see it. "Why would you ask me that?" she asks testily. "Did he say something?"

"No." I watch in the wing mirror as the Plymouth switches lanes. As it speeds past our truck, I catch a glimpse of the driver's middle finger. "I was just wondering."

"We've been apart for thirteen years," she says carefully, her eyes on the road. "Things are different now."

"Because of Samuel?"

Brow furrowed, she shoots me a quick glance. "No, Henry, because of you. Your dad and I work better, *parent* better, as ... friends." Try as I might, I can't make their interactions appear friendly. They are chilly, at best: a chin-tilt through a half-closed car window; a crisply folded note with nary an "x" or "o" ("Henry has a dentist appointment on 9/14, 2:30 p.m. Don't be late again."); and crossed arms, chairs spaced three tiles apart, at parent-teacher conferences.

"Why did you marry Samuel?" I ask as we turn onto the dirt road toward the Campbell farmstead. The truck dips into a pothole, and I bounce out of my seat. "Dad ... doesn't like him." The words spill out as if shaken loose, and I clap my hand over my mouth. I shouldn't have said that.

My mother stops the truck at the closed gate. She opens the driver's side door, letting in a swell of humidity. I expect her to get out and unlatch the gate without answering. It'd give her time to weigh her words, or perhaps, pretend to forget my question. How many times have I walked into a room, forgetting why I'd done it?

Instead, she presses her lips together. "Your dad is ... very sad. Sadness can make us do and say things that aren't very kind."

Her response surprises me. I certainly wouldn't characterize Milton Fairbanks as a sad man. But perhaps sadness likes to disguise itself as anger and ardor. "Why is he sad?" I ask.

"He's always been." Something in my expression must have changed because she reaches out to affectionately jiggle my knee. "Oh honey, it's not because of you. He just is."

"Why don't I make him happy?" My voice wobbles. Embarrassed, I glance out the passenger-side window, swiping at my eyes with my knuckles. *Don't cry, Henry Lee!* Evangeline rubs her fleshy neck against the fence, swatting away mosquitoes with her tail.

"You do," my mother assures me. "He just has a hard time showing it. Sometimes, your dad gets ... lost inside his own head."

I imagine my father sloshing through a murky quagmire, a lantern in hand. The thin beam can't penetrate the dense fog, bouncing back into his eyes. When he cups his hands around his mouth to shout for help, the fog swallows the sound up.

"Is that why you left?" I ask. As soon as I ask the question, I want to ask another: *Why did you make me stay?*

Draping her wrist upon the steering wheel, my mother frowns. "We just didn't work well as husband and wife. That's all." With that, she climbs out of the elevated cab, alighting on the uneven earth with the grace usually afforded to someone wearing much shorter heels.

I know that's not all. But sometimes, adults like to have their secrets.

She unlocks the gate and drags it along its track. It rattles noisily, frightening Evangeline in the neighboring pasture. My mother murmurs something to the animal, but I can't hear her over the pickup's idling engine. When she climbs back into the truck, there's a sheen of sweat on her brow; her blunt bangs stick to her skin. She brushes them off her forehead, and the damp strands stick up like antennae.

"Why Samuel?" I ask again. I am persistent, like a spaniel chasing the bushy tail of a fox through the underbrush. I need to know. My mother is a kindergarten teacher. She packs extra sandwiches in her lunchbox for the students who can't afford the food in the caféteria. It doesn't make sense that she's gotten tangled up with evil incarnate. I can't imagine her at the Black Masses that Father Ricci has described: naked and swaying, gnawing on a rubbery heart, still warm from its sacrificial host. When I imagine her kneeling on the altar, sigils drawn on her bare flesh with blood, my stomach does a somersault.

"He's a good man," she says, driving through the open gate. She parks alongside the veterinarian's truck. "He was there for me when I felt the most alone in the world, even though I had no right to be. I was never alone 'cause you were in my belly." She grins at me.

But I'm not looking at her. Over her shoulder, I can see Samuel and the veterinarian, Dr. Mackie, rounding the side of the house. Both men are perspiring, with blood up to their elbows. Samuel raises his arm to wipe at his damp brow with his shirt sleeve. Even from a distance, I can see the mosquitos buzzing around the pair. "No," I gasp, reaching blindly for my door handle. "No, no, no!"

I bolt from the truck, running past the two men. Samuel calls my name and reaches for me, but his fingertips barely brush against my arm. The chickens scatter as I barrel through the yard; even the rooster, Drumstick, has the good sense to get out of my way. I can see Alban's palomino coat through the slats in the round pen. In the sunshine, he looks golden.

Alban lays on his side in the round pen, his lead rope, still attached, a zig-zag in the dirt. Bright red blood pools under his backside, already beginning to coagulate into a gelatinous sludge. Mosquitos congregate in his open eyes and wide, pink nostrils. I throw my arms over his midsection, pressing my face into his coat and inhaling his horsey smell. Before, Alban merely tolerated my clumsy hugs, his skin twitching beneath my cheek. Now, though, he is motionless.

Samuel rests his forearms on the gate. "I'm sorry," he murmurs. "We couldn't stop the bleeding. It happens sometimes—the blood doesn't clot quick enough." There's a bit of red on his cheek, but it's not blood. It's my mother's lipstick. I imagine her pressing her lips to his weathered, sun-warmed skin, urging him to come to comfort me. The devil must have to be reminded to act human, sometimes. He is a master of disguise, but not, it seems, a purveyor of human emotion.

I run my hands over Alban's dusty coat, my palms bumping over the ridges of his ribcage. "You killed him," I grumble, through gritted teeth. The mosquitos tangle in my hair, their gossamer wings beating against my skin. My blood must be more appealing than Alban's.

"Henry—" Samuel comes through the gate. He squeezes my shoulder. "You don't mean that."

"You killed him," I roar, pushing him away with both hands. I'm not strong, but he stumbles back in surprise. "And I'll kill *you!*"

Wharton, Virginia—Present Day

Despite using half-doses, I've run out of ketamine. I toss the last empty vial into the bathroom trash can, concealing it with a wad of toilet paper. Cordelia will be a very real problem within the next few hours unless I can find some way to put a leash on her.

It's dark in the room, the heavy curtains drawn across the windows. Dimly, I can hear jangly calliope music wafting up from the boardwalk. Cordelia dozes atop the bedspread, a trickle of blood edging down her deltoid. I must have inadvertently nicked a capillary while administering the last dose. She's been wearing the same clothes for three days now, and they are wrinkled, sweat staining the silk.

My revolver rests on the desk, just where I had left it. The bullets jingle in my jacket pocket. If I jam a pillow between the muzzle and Cordelia's head, no one will hear the gunshot. I may even spare myself the sight of blood and brain. Instead, I pace. "She's not your sister," I mutter to myself. "She's the devil's daughter." No matter how much I repeat it, I can't quite convince myself. She has our mother's dimpled chin and prosodic tone, and our mother was an angel.

At the sound of my voice, Cordelia stirs. Her hair sticks to her cheek, made damp by her drool. "Thirsty," she rasps.

"First we're going to talk," I say, pulling out the rolling chair tucked under the secretary-style desk. Airless potato chip bags, empty coffee cups, and two bottles of Deer Park, refilled from the bathroom tap, litter the desktop. I unscrew the plastic cap on one of the bottles, taking a hearty swig. The stale water tastes faintly of chlorine. Still, I make it look appetizing, smacking my lips as though I've just drank directly from a mountain spring. Cordelia watches me, her tongue dragging along her dry lips. The ketamine makes her droughty.

"We're going to go back to that café and follow that girl. She'll lead us to Haley." I prop my feet up on the bed, not bothering to take off my shoes. Fearful, Cordelia curls up like a fawn in a nest of clover. I wonder, not for the first time, what phantasmagoria the ketamine has created for my sister. With every subsequent dose, she looks more harried, her eyes flitting like a prey animal's. Surely, she's never felt this way before; her place on the food chain is a throne. Do the treads on my boots resemble the pebbled skin of Komodo dragons or the scales of anacondas?

"I'm here to help her," I continue. "She nearly killed someone, Cordy. She'll do it again."

Cordelia reaches out to the water bottle as if it's within her reach. She just looks silly, her fingers waggling in the air. It reminds me of when she was a toddler, begging to be picked up. She loved to be carried around the farmyard on my shoulders, especially when I pretended to gallop. "You ... kidnapped me," she mutters.

141

"A means to an end, nothing more," I reply. Tiring of her whimpering, I toss her the other water bottle. The water inside sloshes; I hope that, to her, it sounds like a swarm of bees. She fumbles with the lid, then greedily gulps from the bottle. The water trickles down both sides of her mouth, but she doesn't seem to notice nor care. "I'm sorry I did it. I shouldn't have. But if you had warned her, she'd have run."

She drinks until the bottle is empty, the plastic crinkling. "You don't know my daughter. She wouldn't run from me."

"Are you sure about that, Cordy? She left town after ripping off a woman's leg. I've seen your phone: hundreds of unreturned calls and texts." I paw through the mess on the desk, finding her ruined iPhone. The screen is cracked, and the bevel bent, courtesy of my boot. I toss it onto the bed. "My favorite text was: 'Haley, the ladies at Bunco keep asking about you. Call me.' It's no wonder she doesn't want to be found."

My sister flings the empty Deer Park bottle in my direction. It bounces off of the desk, rolling beneath the pleated bed skirt. "Why are you doing this?" she moans. It's not the first time she's asked the question, nor the first time I've answered it. The ketamine makes her forgetful. It's meant to. Often—far more often than one would expect—patients in surgery wake up, finding themselves the star of a macabre game of show and tell. *This is my lower intestine; it is very long like a snake! It absorbs nutrients.* After the oft-startled anesthesiologist pushes more meds, the patient promptly forgets the smell of their cauterizing bowel or the burn of the ventilator in their windpipe.

I slide the revolver off the desktop and into my lap, scooping a small handful of bullets from my pocket. One by one, I load them into their respective chamber, pulling down the hammer. The tendon in my thumb twangs painfully, and I drop the loaded gun into my lap so that I can massage the abductor muscle. The cold weather is not kind to my hands. "Did they ever tell you what happened in 1970? Did you even notice I was gone?"

"Mom said your dad abducted you." With a little groan, Cordelia sits up in bed. Her limp, greasy hair hangs over her face. "She went to pick you up after weekend visitation and the house was empty."

I laugh at the lie. "No, my dad died that summer. Maybe Samuel didn't pull the trigger, but he was the one who *killed* him. I ran away."

Cordelia frowns. "No," she mutters, "that's not right."

"You were a little girl. Only six," I murmur soothingly. Resting my hand on the pommel of the revolver, I stroke it like a pet. "I ran away to a cabin in Montana. It was a little a-frame with no heat, and I can still remember the long, cold walk to the woodshed. I had to carry a rifle because of the bears."

Wordlessly, Cordelia shakes her head. "My dad wouldn't—"

"Your dad was a killer, Cordy. He wrote all about it in his diary. I have the book right here." I jerk my thumb at my duffel bag, resting beside the ticking radiator. "If I had done what I was supposed to do, I could have stayed. I could have broken an entire chain of events that ended with your daughter chewing up innocent girls."

Groaning, Cordelia presses the heels of her hands into her eye sockets. Her head must hurt terribly. "What were you supposed to do?" she asks warily.

I ignore the question. "I'm going to stop Haley before she hurts anyone else, and you're going to help me."

Cordelia laughs. It's a humorless, monosyllabic bark. "You really think I'll help you?"

"I don't have to think anything," I reply coolly. "I know you will. If you don't, hellfire will rain down upon all of your heads. I'm not the only lamb in the flock, Cordy. If I say the word, a bullet will find a new home in your husband's head while he's having his grapefruit in the morning. Your husband has a sister too, right? She has twins at Ridgerton Elementary, who go out for recess at 11:35 and play hopscotch."

It's a lie, of course. I have no accomplices. But it does the trick. Cordelia hyperventilates like a dog trapped in a hot car. "No, no," she whimpers.

"This is basic math, sis. What is worth more: one life or many?" I scratch an itch at my temple with the revolver's front sight.

Cordelia lurches at me, the sheets shredding as her nails grow into scythe-like claws. When she pulls her lips away from her teeth, they are sharp and numerous. Her powerful back legs acting like pistons, she leaps off the bed, knocking my chair backward. We fall together onto the thin carpet. The chairback shatters on impact, a splinter jabbing into my ribs. My sister's face is inches from mine now, a disturbing amalgamation of wolf and housewife. Her rosy skin is stretched tight over a hairless snout, the pores enlarged to accommodate whiskers. I press the barrel of the gun against her forehead. "Bang," I say, her snarls reverberating through my chest wall.

CHAPTER 14
(ANGUS)

———◁◆▷———

I pull my scrub pants up over my ass, tying the drawstring with nimble fingers. Hunter is already dressed, his hand resting on the doorknob. He nibbles at his lip. "We still need to talk," he reminds me. "About everything."

I wince. *Everything.* I imagine stretching the entirety of our relationship out on a surgeon's table and excising the warts. I wonder what will be healthy enough to keep. "I know," I say.

Still, Hunter doesn't open the door. "I still want to—"

"I know," I interrupt. "Hunter, I *know.* But we can't talk about it in this closet." I can't find my badge. It must have fallen off. I crouch, stuffing my fingers beneath the shelving unit and wiging them around. I touch something sticky.

"We did plenty of things in this closet," he reminds me.

There! My fingers butt against a bit of plastic, and I manage to pinch it between my index and middle fingers. I brush away a dust bunny before clipping it back onto my lapel. "I promise we'll talk," I assure him before pressing my lips against the corner of his mouth. "Tonight. I'll come over."

"You'll come home?" he asks hopefully, bouncing on his toes.

"I'll come home."

I open the door and make a beeline down the hall. Compared to the closet, it is dazzlingly bright, and I have to squint until my eyes adjust. Hunter follows more slowly, his cheeks ruddy. Every time a nurse passes by, he ducks his head, avoiding their eyes. He thinks everyone on the unit overheard our lovemaking. Even if they had, they wouldn't bat an eye. It certainly wouldn't be the first time someone fucked in that closet.

Candy and Haley are still in the waiting room. They sit across from one another, playing footsie in the aisle. A Rankin/Bass Christmas film is on television, Rudolph's reedy voice trickling through the speakers. A child wearing an "I'm a Big Sister!" shirt hums along to "A Holly Jolly Christmas" while an older man dozes, his chin in his palm.

Haley looks up as we approach, her eyebrows invading her hairline. "Where have you two been?" she asks. "Hunter, you look ... sweaty."

There is an oily sheen on Hunter's brow. The shadow of a suck mark adorns his throat. I would like to watch him navigate what promises to be an awkward conversation, but we've been gone too long. "Any word from Ama?" I ask.

"She stepped out while Toby was being helped to the bathroom," Candy says, though her eyes remain on her bashful brother. "She wants to see you."

I consider leaving Hunter to the sharks, but they can smell chum in the water. They'll devour him. I urge him to follow me to Toby's room. He is so relieved at the invitation that he nearly steps on my heels.

The room is dim, sunlight trickling through the slats in the blinds. Ama sits in an armchair at Toby's bedside, holding the young woman's hand. "When will they let me see him?" Toby asks as soon as we enter. She is restless, not unlike a tiger pacing its enclosure.

"Soon," I assure her, though "soon" in a hospital is relative. It could mean minutes or hours. "They just want to make sure you are both stable first."

Toby groans, scratching at a bit of adhesive left on her chest. "I'm fine." She throws her head back against the thin pillow, her braids fanning out around her head like a halo. "I just want to see him."

"Soon," Ama echoes, patting her hand.

Hunter sidesteps around me, leaning over to kiss the frustrated girl on the cheek. "I heard you broke into my café," he teases.

Toby's eyes widen at the sight of him. "I haven't seen the two of you in the same room since Thanksgiving," she squeals. "Did I make this happen?"

Thankfully, before she can make a big deal out of it, Dr. Henrikson knocks on the doorframe. We've never met, but he is a favorite of the hospital grapevine. If Wharton Med was the set of a primetime drama, he would be the main character. "Good morning, mom," he says cheerily. "I'm Dr. Henrikson. I just got the chance to meet your little guy."

Toby sits up, nearly wrenching out the intravenous line taped to the back of her hand. "Is he okay?"

"Mr. Asher is doing fantastic. He's breathing on his own and his temperature is stable. I was just coming to see if you'd like to try giving him some milk." He gestures into the hall where a nurse waits with a wheelchair. "If so, your chariot awaits."

"Yes!" Toby throws her legs over the side of the bed, reaching for the I.V. pole. While the exertion makes her pale and breathless, her clenched teeth is a dare. We all know better than to ask her to take a beat. The nurse helps her transfer into the wheelchair.

"Unfortunately, we can only take mom and one support person," Dr. Henrikson says, rubbing his dry hands together.

"Ama," Toby's fingers brush against the older woman's arm as she is wheeled past.

"I'll be right behind you," Ama assures her ward. Reaching for her cane, she rises, shuffling after the retinue and its I.V pole banner. I notice then that she is wearing her house slippers. What I assumed was a cardigan is, in all actuality, her dressing gown. Ama pauses in the doorway, turning to look at Hunter and me. "Perhaps our luck is finally changing," she says with a toothy smile.

♦ ♦ ♦

I drive Hunter home so that he doesn't have to ride on the bench seat in Haley's pickup. It's cramped for three adults, sitting cheek-to-jowl. The girls' truck tails us down Main, though I wish Haley would have taken the lead. She's impatient, riding my bumper like she's late for something.

While Hunter and I ride in silence, there's no weight to it; it's comfortable. Despite the cold, Hunter rolls down the window in my car. The wind lashes against his cheeks, turning him rosy. I desperately want to pull over and kiss his icy skin. Instead, I rest my hand on his bouncing knee. He's been nervous in the car since the crash. Whenever I roll over a speed bump or inadvertently bounce into a pothole, he squeezes his eyes shut and grips the armrests with both hands.

When we pass the Ebb and Flow storefront on Main, he averts his eyes and hums. I catch a brief glimpse of the workmen inside hanging drywall. The echo of hammers wafts through the open window, and Hunter rolls it back up.

When we reach Bird's Nest, his knuckles regain their color. His shoulders, taut around his ears for the entire trip, sag. "You'll come over tonight?" he asks hopefully, no longer needing to hold his breath. I wonder, not for the first time, why Bird's Nest feels safe. Surely, it's not because of me. Will I ever not feel guilty for bringing stress into his quiet life, like shit stuck to my shoe?

"Yeah," I reply, though I should say, *No, I'd better not*. If I was a better man, I'd leave him alone. Surely, it's selfish to love someone so much that you can't be without them. Though love is, by its very nature, self-serving, isn't it? I wonder, not for the first time, whether I'm balking at his ultimatum because a wolfish boyfriend doesn't benefit me. With Hunter, I can pretend to be human. If only —

Suddenly, a blond woman stumbles out of the reeds and into the road. She falls to her knees in the gravel, her hands clasped as if in prayer. "What the fuck?" I exclaim, slamming on the brakes and cranking the wheel to avoid hitting her. My sedan careens into the ditch, and the airbag punches me in the chest. *Oomph*. Before I can take stock of the situation, the car lurches forward, the front end crumpling against the concrete culvert. Haley's truck fills my rearview mirror. She swerved too.

I push the spent airbag away. It burnt my forearm, leaving the skin raw and leaking sebum. "Hunter, are you alright?" I ask, reaching across the center console to touch him.

Hunter trembles. Even his cheeks, freckled with sodium azide, tremble. "Who was that?" he manages. "W-w-why did she run into the road?"

"I'm going to make sure everyone's okay," I say, taking off my seatbelt. When I climb out of the car, I step directly into water. It floods my shoes and socks, numbing my toes. Scrambling up the embankment, I am keenly aware of a swath of soreness that extends from my right shoulder to left hip. The seat belt did its job.

Hunter follows me out of the driver's side door. "My door won't open," he mumbles. He sloshes through the water. I reach down to help him up the steep embankment, gritting my teeth at the sear in my shoulder.

151

"Mom?" Haley lurches out of her truck, her eyes on the kneeling woman. Hunter wraps Haley in a bear hug. "It's not safe," he insists. "Look at her hands."

The woman struggles to regain her feet, wobbling toward us. Blood stains her pant leg; she'd split her knee open when she fell. Her hands aren't clasped in prayer, but bound with a dingy shoelace, the aglet fraying. "Run!" she screams.

The gunshot startles the seagulls roosting on Hunter's bungalow. A flurry of feathers and bird shit bedeck the sun-bleached shingles. The woman freezes, her arms awkwardly thrown over her head. I scan the culverts across the road, searching for a shooter kneeling amidst the cattails, but there's no one there. I sniff, but the wind is at my back. I can only smell the crisp, brackish air pouring off the ocean.

"Angus—" Hunter's voice is a wet croak.

Hunter's hands slowly slide off of Haley's arms. The unwieldy weight of him on her back causes Haley to pitch forward. For a brief moment, Hunter's chin rests on the girl's shoulder, his eyes unfocused and glassy, as though he is deep in thought. "Ang—" he mumbles, coughing up a bubble of blood.

"Hunter!" I barely manage to catch him before he falls, landing on my butt in the loose gravel. With his head in my lap, I unzip his jacket, searching for a wound. There's a small hole in his t-shirt. At first, I mistake it for wear and tear from the washer. He never throws away clothes, whether they are stained, moth-eaten, or holey. But then, blood gurgles through the fabric. I clap my hands over the wound.

Candy grabs fistfuls of my jacket, trying to pull Hunter and I back down the embankment. "We have to hide," she sobs. She's right. I grab Hunter by the armpits, scooting toward the ditch on my butt. Together, we tumble into the stream and the water turns pink.

Free of Hunter's embrace, Haley sprints toward her mother. She grabs her by the forearm, tugging her toward our side of the road. The second shot rings out just as Haley slides down the embankment. A cattail explodes, shedding fluffy seeds.

Hunter is shivering, whether from the chilly water or shock, I can't be certain. His eyes are closed, the eyelids smooth as though he's in the middle of a dreamless sleep. "Hunter?" I call. "Can you hear me?" He doesn't stir.

Candy squats in the water beside me, fumbling with her bag. She pulls out her phone, cursing when the screen doesn't acknowledge her damp fingertaps. Wiping her hands on her shirt, she tries again, managing to dial 9-1-1. I can dimly hear the operator's voice on the line and Candy's harried, "I'm at 133 Bird's Nest. My brother has been shot in the chest. No, no, we don't know where the shooter is."

Haley picks at the shoelace knotted around her mother's wrists, trying to release her. "Who did this?" she asks. "How did you get here?" The woman only blubbers, snot and tears making her skin shiny.

But I don't care who did this. I just want Hunter to open his eyes. *Please.*

CHAPTER 15
(HUNTER)

"Wake up, Hunter," Angus croons.

"Mmm!" I protest, pulling the down comforter over my head. "Five more minutes, please." It is so quiet in the room that I assume he has been swayed by my entreaty. After all, I've been working twelve-hour days, six days a week, for much of December. Capitalism: 'tis the reason for the season.

The mattress dips under Angus' weight as he sits on the corner. "It's Christmas," he wheedles, giving my thigh a hearty shake. "We've got to open presents."

"We're adults. We can open presents whenever we'd like. Five more minutes." With the luxuriant comforter over my head, I'm getting overheated and breathless, but I don't dare surface. The sun is up, and if I get so much as a peek at it, I'll be hopelessly awake.

Angus' fingers walk up my hip. "Wake up, Hunter." I can hear the smile in his voice. He thinks he's being playful, and that I am being coy.

Bristling, I bat his hand away. "Just let me sleep!"

The mattress shifts as he straddles my cocoon. "C'mon!" he cajoles, bouncing so that the whole bed-frame rattles. The headboard slaps the wall. "We just want you to open your eyes."

Agitation gives way to anger. He's being obstinate now, and for what? I haven't asked for much. I never ask for much. I throw off the comforter, pushing him. "Why can't you just fucking listen?"

But it's not Angus at all. James Volkov crouches on my chest like an incubus, his mouth stretched into something that a more generous person would call a smile, that is, if he still had a lower jaw. His tongue lolls, coating his chin in slobber. His face is largely unrecognizable; purple swelling engulfs his nose and angular cheekbones and his once piercing eyes are milky and leaking aqueous humor. I recognize him because of the Haniya mask tattooed on his throat. "Wake up," he garbles.

"N-n-no, no, no," I stammer. I push on his chest, but he is as immovable as an elm tree. His skin is damp, as is his stringy hair. As he shakes his head, foul-smelling droplets pepper the comforter. He smells like a marsh— sulfurous and pungent. James tilts his head. The vertebrae pop one by one. Crick-crick-crick.

"What do you think?" Toby asks.

I'm sitting on the couch now, still wearing my flannel pajama pants. My t-shirt is damp, clinging to my skin. "What?" I manage.

"The tree!" She gestures like Vanna White at the Christmas tree. It is a squat fir, the needles dusted with a white powder meant to give the impression of

snowfall. While it is decorated with red and gold baubles, there's something dreary about it.

"You forgot the lights," I point out.

"Oh." Toby frowns at the tree. She's still wearing her hospital gown, her braids piled on her head in a row of Bantu knots. "The hospital wouldn't let us plug it in." When she puts her hands on her hips, the twill tape keeping the back of her hospital gown modest loosens.

"Well, I like it," Leigh Volkov says. She sits on the couch beside me, her body twisted like a pretzel. Her skin is dirt-streaked. When she moves, her dress crinkles; it's just a sheet of opaque plastic wrapped around her midsection.

"Why are you here?" I moan. It is difficult to look at her, though I can't seem to drag my eyes away. Her broken arm rests across her scapula, the fingers tapping a melody upon her freckled shoulder. It's the jingle from the arcade game Luka played at Freddie's on the day of the bonfire. It was Leigh who ushered me into this world, wasn't it? If she had not invited me to Freddie's, Angus and I would have passed each other by like ships in the night.

"It's Christmas," Leigh says. Her stiff, bloodless lips twitch. "I'm the ghost of Christmas Past."

"I don't know where I am," I admit, my voice wobbling. Hot tears brim in my eyes. I feel off-kilter like I've been dropped upon an M.C Escher staircase and told to find the landing. Which way is up?

"Do you want to wake up?" Leigh asks. There's a tenderness to her voice that I've never heard before. She pities me.

My stomach tips over, and I'm standing on the beach. Sizzling stomach acid sloshes up my esophagus. The sand shifts beneath my bare feet. I'm standing beneath the boardwalk, dwarfed by its concrete-encased pylons. Someone tagged the nearest support, the lettering slapdash and dripping. W4 K€ ØP! I can't decipher what it means.

Overhead, the boardwalk bustles. Even the roar of the ocean cannot drown out the strangely euphonic melody of "Last Christmas." Under the shadow of the boardwalk, it is cold. I rub at my arms, pebbled with gooseflesh. It is far too cold to be outside in pajama pants and a damp t-shirt.

The ocean is sluggish, the waves seemingly trapped under a layer of permafrost. I wonder what it would be like to walk on top of it. Would I ever reach the horizon, where the brackish sea meets the ash-colored sky? I take a few stumbling steps toward the breakers, propelled by a tugging sensation in my sternum.

"Hunter!" Angus calls. "Come back to me." His voice floats down from the boardwalk.

He sounds too far away. The ocean is much closer. My toes dip into the sea foam. I expect a chill, but the cold is unfathomable. It seeps into my bones, numbing my extremities. I take another step, the water lapping at my ankles.

Someone grabs my shirt collar, pulling me back. At first, I don't recognize her. She is smaller than I remember, and her hair is a bird's nest made wild by the wind. When I last saw her, she was bald. "Mom?" I manage.

157

She smiles. When she was in the midst of chemo-therapy, her teeth were yellowing, the gumline thick with plaque. Now, they are dazzlingly white. Her once sunken cheeks are rosy, dimpled apples. "Hunter, my sweet boy."

Her voice makes me want to cry. I'd forgotten what she sounded like. In my memories, her voice had taken on the staticky, low-pitched quality of a VHS tape. After all, it was all we had of her: spools of vid-eotape, degrading in a cardboard box. In reality, her voice is sweet and lilting, as soothing as a hammock in late spring.

She cups my face in her cool hands. "You have to wake up. It's Christmas." When she kisses my forehead, I take my first breath.

CHAPTER 16
(ANGUS)

———◁◆▷———

H unter gags as Dr. Fitzsimmons pulls the endotracheal tube from his throat. His eyes bulge.
The lidocaine tempers his urge to cough, so he simply
groans. It reminds me of his exasperated moan when
the alarm goes off before sunrise. *Already?*

I squeeze his hand, wanting him to know he isn't
alone. When the tube finally breaches his jaws, he
quiets and closes his eyes. The doctor threads a can-
nula beneath his nostrils, tucking it behind his ears.
"You know the drill," Dr. Fitzsimmons says. "Third
time's the charm."

Glancing warily at the pulse oximeter, I nibble at
my lip. "Third time's the charm," I repeat. The words
taste like ash on my tongue.

Dr. Fitzsimmons unties the shoulder of Hunter's
gown, folding it down to reveal a thick square bandage upon his chest. Carefully, he picks at the adhesive,
pulling it away from the healing wound. "Looking
good," he says. I'm not entirely sure I agree; the

wound, held closed by bristly sutures, looks angry. The skin is red and mottled.

"No more infection?" I ask hopefully.

"I'm still waiting for the results from the lab," he replies. He smooths the bandage back into place with gentle, practiced hands. "They are slow down there without you," he adds with a wink.

Detective Acker knocks on the doorframe. He holds a paper mask against his mustachioed mouth as if afraid gunshots are infectious. The musky cologne he wears pours into the room before him like a phalanx of soldiers. The smell gives me a headache, the citrusy undertones burning the hair from my nostrils. "Can I come in?" he asks, though I know it's not a question. I nod, gesturing to the empty chair usually occupied by Hunter's sister as if to say, *Be my guest*.

"We're all done here," the doctor says, snapping off his gloves. "For now." The caveat sounds ominous. It's a reminder: this can all go sideways, as it has done twice before. *Don't get your hopes up, Angus*. He collects a dollop of hand sanitizer on the way out, humming that annoying Wham! tune he seems to love.

The detective sits heavily, letting out a sigh. "How is he?"

"Breathing on his own," I say, reaching for Hunter's limp hand resting atop the blankets. "Again." I look warily at the pulse oximeter: 94%. "C'mon, Hunt," I mutter under my breath.

"You look like shit," Acker observes. "Have you been getting any rest?"

"I'm fine." I release Hunter's hand, leaning back in my chair. My hip flexor twangs. The pulse oximeter reads 95%. Perhaps the third time's the charm, after all. "I need to be here."

The detective pulls his notepad out of his pocket, clicking the top of his pen to reveal the nib. He scribbles in the corner of the empty page as if to assure himself that the pen is functional. "Tell me what happened—everything you remember."

"We were driving home from the hospital. My ... niece ... just had a baby."

"Ah yes, the baby delivered in the café you broke into," Acker says snidely. "You were the talk of the town at The Dock." The Dock is a tumbledown bar on Lewis Street where cops and their ilk drink for free. It's a favorite of the sailors stationed in Norfolk.

"I didn't break in." *Only technically,* I amend.

Acker writes something, but I can't quite read it. There's a certain sharpness to his penmanship, as though he's writing with a rapier. The arm on the A and crossbar on the T are overly long, crowding the neighboring letters. "Continue," he finally says.

"We were on Bird's Nest, and a woman jumped out in front of the car. I swerved to avoid her." The pulse oximeter plunges to 92%, and I lean forward, elbows on my knees. I stare at Hunter's face, searching for any signs of distress: a furrowed brow, a bluish tinge to the lips, sweat that turns his hospital gown a dingy gray. He only lets out a soft sigh, as if dreaming about something particularly sumptuous—or heartbreaking.

Detective Acker flips the page of his notebook, reading what he'd written. "Cordelia Campbell."

I shift in my chair. Cordelia Campbell is staying at Hunter's bungalow with Haley and Candy. The detective must have been there to interview her. The thought of the detective sitting on Hunter's couch makes me uneasy. "That's right," I finally say.

The pulse oximeter drops to 91% and lets out a panicked *beep*. I sandwich Hunter's hand between both of mine, hoping he can feel me there. He's been unconscious for most of the last week, but he's stirred once or twice, murmuring around the endotracheal tube.

"She says she was kidnapped by a man called Henry Fairbanks." Acker is oblivious to the alarm's meaning. It sounds innocuous. But it's the first chirp of a dying fire alarm before the spark on the stovetop. It is a portent. "That he was the one who shot Mr. Bailey."

"I didn't see the shooter." 90%. I slowly rise from my chair. My fingers twitch. *Should I push the call button?*

"Why do you think he was shooting at you?"

"I don't know," I admit.

"He's your roommate's uncle," the detective says. "I mean, she's *Hunter's* roommate. You don't live there anymore, do you?"

I give him a sharp look. He is impassive, his eyes half-lidded. I can't tell if that was meant to be a barb or simply a statement of fact. "I was moving back in," I snap. At least, I had hoped I was. During that fateful car ride, I felt so hopeful. Where there was a dark void, the future I saw with Hunter Bailey had rematerialized. In that future, he lies beside me in our shared bed, his cheek pillowed on my shoulder. His hand rests amidst a tangle of my chest hair, the cool metal of his ring raising a patch of gooseflesh. I never got the opportunity to give it to him.

"We found his car," he says, tapping the end cap of his pen against his chin. "Parked just off Clementine Ave. D'ya know what we found in his trunk?"

"No. Why would I?"

"We found empty vials of Ketaset. D'ya know what that's for?"

"I'm not a doctor," I say coolly. I don't like the detective's tone. It feels as though he's laying a trap, waiting for me to sniff at the bait. It doesn't make sense. Aren't we the victims here?

"A veterinarian, actually. It's liquid ketamine, used to anesthetize dogs. But Henry Fairbanks isn't a vet. He's just some Geek Squad technician at a Best Buy out in Montana. He doesn't even have a dog."

"Fascinating," I say, though I'm only half-listening. The pulse oximeter is still at 90%, straddling the line it can't cross. If Hunter has to go back on the ventilator, we may never get him off. The future I'd envisioned grows hazy around the edges. A new future—a tracheostomy, endless surgeries, a gravestone of polished granite—materializes.

"I just find it strange," Detective Acker muses. "Considering where we live. I'm sure you've heard the stories."

I whirl to face him, impatient. "Shouldn't you be out there looking for this guy? Isn't that your fucking job?" Paresthesia prickles on the back of my neck.

Unflappable, the detective continues. "Did you ever hear about Freddy Parnell? He killed six people back in the late 1940s, got the electric chair in 1993. That's a long time to sit on death row, but he kept appealing. Said he didn't do it. Pleaded mental incompetency and everything."

"I remember." Everyone does. Parnell's name is often spoken in the same breath as Ted Bundy, Ed Kemper, and Jeffrey Dahmer. There are countless podcasts about him. I was only six when he was executed, but his mugshot was a near-constant fixture on the television that summer. I was visiting Ama, and we would sit in front of the oscillating fan in her living room, watching daytime television and sucking on dripping popsicles to beat the heat. Freddy Parnell was presented as a man of two faces: a young man standing outside The Dock's phone booth, a fluffy cat standing on his shoulders, and an old man with vacant eyes, wearing prison orange. Every time he appeared on-screen, Ama would reach for the remote or get up to shuffle into the kitchen. Once, I caught her sniffling, on the phone with a friend. "I wish we could stop this, Flora. Are you certain there's no way?"

"I got to see those old files. I was curious, 'cause my daddy worked the case. I found his signature on the arrest record: Sheriff Lyle Acker. The autopsy pictures are somethin' else. They don't look like the work of a man at all but a dog. They were absolutely shredded."

"I saw the 20/20 episode."

"I saw somethin' interesting in that file. One of the victims, Lucy Carson, was staying at a shitty little motel called The Cove. D'ya know who owned it?" Before I can answer, he blurts it out like a child who can't wait to tell a secret. "Rafe Blanchard, *your* grandfather."

"My family has roots here, same as yours."

"Just funny, is all. The connection." He idly clicks the pen cap.

"I'm not sure I see one." I shrug. He's definitely laying a trap. I can almost see the noose on the ground, buried in leaf litter. If I misstep, he'll pull it tight around my ankles. I feel much too unsteady for this game of cat-and-mouse. The pulse oximeter beeps, dropping again to 89%. Dimly, I am aware of frantic voices outside. The nurses are coming.

Abruptly, Hunter opens his eyes. They are a brilliant green, reminiscent of summers lolling in the grass on a gingham blanket. However, now, I can only think of the foul-smelling algae in the culvert, making the concrete walls slick and the water muculent. It is the color of infection. "Hunter?" I whisper, licking at my dry lips.

Hunter's eyes slide up toward the ceiling and his body jerks. The spasmodic movements are so violent that the bed shakes. "Fuck!" the detective shouts, leaping to his feet. He runs to the door, throwing it open. "Nurse! *Nurse!*"

I am rooted in place. Blood trickles out of the corners of Hunter's mouth. He's bitten his tongue. His arms tangle in his sheets. "Move!" Detective Acker grabs my arm, pulling me back as a cavalcade of nurses rush into the room. *Fwump.* Hunter's bed flattens, and someone pulls the pillow out from beneath his head. Hands sheathed in latex gloves probe his skin. What if it's the last thing he feels? A sob erupts from my throat; it feels like violence, a knife slicing my airway into ribbons.

Hunter!

♦ ♦ ♦

I crest the hill just as the first snowflake alights upon my fur. A few more errant flakes follow, leaving wet splotches upon my snout and the water tower's rust-caked pylons. It's too warm to snow outright, but the flurry is its own knife buried deep inside my gut. "Maybe we'll have a white Christmas," Hunter had said just before Thanksgiving, peeling the curtain away from the window to study the clouds overhead.

He looked at snow with the wide-eyed astonishment of a child. He'd pinned travel advertisements featuring Mount Tremblant on his wall in his early teens, desperate to learn how to ski. The dream was never realized because there was a café to manage and an ailing mother to care for. If he were able, he'd be standing out on the deck with his chin tilted skyward, waiting for a snowflake to alight on his tongue.

In the shade offered by the poplar trees, the temperature drops five degrees. In my human flesh, it would be uncomfortable, but, wolfish, it is pleasant, thanks to my wooly undercoat. The chill sucks the tears from my eyes, yet, for that, I am grateful. If I cry, I am certain that all of the moisture will vacate my body, leaving me desiccated and crumbly. Dust unto dust. I break into a jog, waiting for my taut muscles to loosen. I am desperate to run until I am panting so that I can expel all of the despair trapped in my lungs. It will feel good for it to float away like vapor.

This afternoon, Dr. Fitzsimmons escorted Candy and me into one of the hospital's family rooms. The name is a misnomer; the room isn't meant to comfort the family but rather to keep the rest of the patient population docile. It's the serpentine chute in a slaughterhouse, keeping the cows from seeing the bolt until it's too late. The vinyl of the couch stuck to my skin, and the potted plant on the end table, meant to make the space inviting, was brown and brittle. I heard very little beyond, *I'm sorry to have to tell you this, but...*

Candy cried, wiping at her snotty nose with the sleeves of her cardigan. She parroted the doctor's words back to him, as if hoping she'd misheard him. She tapped keywords into the notes app on her iPhone: Propofol, tracheostomy, sepsis. The last word skitters through my brain like a millipede. Sssepssiss—the infection he got because I dragged him into the culvert. Why hadn't I run after the shooter instead? Hunter's pleading eyes kept me beside him, his twitching fingers clutching at my shirtfront.

I lope through the forest, my head slung low. Despite the cold, I catch the pungent stench of a buck, a mile upwind. It's reckless and foolhardy to approach on my own, but I am unburdened by self-preservation.

I track the buck to a half-frozen creek; chunks of ice, moved by the current, noisily crash against the craggy rocks jutting out of the crystal-clear water. The ground is thick with decaying leaves, and they crunch beneath the buck's hooves. The 300-pound animal drinks from the creek, his crown of antlers throwing shadows over his flattened brow. A tatter of shed velvet still clings to one of the prongs, flapping like a banner of war. After drinking his fill, he rubs his antlers against a nearby maple, scraping the flaky bark off of the trunk. Beneath the bark, the trunk is red like blood.

It is only when I rest upon my belly to watch him that I realize that I've run all the way to the parcel of forest that butts up against Bird's Nest. Mushrooms with wide, flat caps flourish in the shade beneath the maples here, rooted in concentric circles. Faerie rings, they call them. It's very near where I buried Leigh Volkov.

Suddenly, the buck snaps his wedge-shaped head in my direction. Our eyes meet, and he turns tail, crashing through the underbrush. I follow, desperate for the euphoria that only a surge of adrenaline can offer. It's as potent as a shot of Jameson, gulped sloppily from the bottle. The buck leaps over the tower of stones marking Leigh's grave, his cloven hoof tapping the uppermost stone. The marker topples over.

At the gravesite, I pause. There's a furrow in the earth, as though someone started to dig but thought better of it.

A glint of metal amidst the bracken catches my eye. It's a black fountain pen, the clip a shiny silver. The plastic hasn't eroded, though it is damp. It hasn't been here long. In this particular part of the forest, humans are a rarity. In the summer, the ground is overrun with poison sumac. It's unpleasant for humans, but it is a smorgasbord for prey animals. I bring the pen to my snout, giving it a sniff. It smells like cologne, the top note bergamot.

Detective Acker was here.

CHAPTER 17
(HENRY)

————⊲◆⊳————

Sevierville, Tennessee—August 1970

The humidity makes it hard to breathe, much less run. I may as well be swimming through a thick chowder, swallowing huge gulps of it in lieu of fresh air. Sweat soaks through the band of my Sevierville Swallowtails baseball cap and drips into my eyes. I imagine cartoony stink lines wafting off my back. I smell foul; the dogs will have no trouble tracking my stench. If I can't conceal it, they'll come right for me, their white-tipped tails wagging and bodies trembling in excitement.

In the distance, I can hear them yipping and yodeling. For them, this is a game with a prize at the end. For me, this is as close to life or death as one can get. If I fail this trial—one of many conducted over the last two weekends—I'll be a good-for-nothing in the eyes of my father. That, I'm convinced, will be worse than death. His cruelty will be untempered. The tiny moments of coziness—a pat on the shoulder, a side-long hug—will be no more.

I've passed the other trials. I'm a decent shot, and I memorized every passage in the Bible relating to evil and its myriad forms. Admittedly, the verses, learned by rote, were supposed to make my purpose clear, but they only served to confuse me further. All of the passages seemed to be forbidding my father's every action: his hardheartedness, his love of booze, and his hankering to cast the first stone. When I asked Father Ricci about it, he merely waved the question away like smoke. "'We see through a mirror, darkly,'" he recited, in the mellifluous tone he reserved only for recitation. "Do you know what that means, Henry?" When I shook my head, he steepled his fingers beneath his chin. "It means we can only know what we know, no more. You just have to have faith in what you can see."

I skitter through a field, powerlines crisscrossing overhead, then crash through a thick swath of black-berry bushes. The brambles cut up the bare skin of my arms. The berries that have fallen underfoot stain my shoes purple. I have a vague idea of where I am and veer due east, listening for the sound of water. With the canopy above, the air feels somewhat cooler, but there are far more mosquitos. They alight on my arms and neck, the pinch of their proboscis promising me an itchy evening.

Through the trees, I catch a glimpse of the sun glancing off of the still, blue water of Red Lynx Reservoir. The water will confuse the dogs and send them skittering along the shoreline, trying to find me again. Elated, I slide down the muddy bank, throwing myself into the clear water. The cold of it is a shock after the hot summer's sun, and I gasp.

The dogs are getting closer. I can hear my father and the priest with them, laughing. "Find it! Find it!" my father loudly commands, his voice as harsh as a cracking whip.

Nearby, I spot a floating dock, bobbing just above the surface of the water. I swim toward it, careful not to splash. The dogs have heavy, floppy ears, but they are keen all the same. Beneath the dock, there's a thin pocket of air. If I tilt my head just so, I can suck the muggy air into my lungs, though it reeks. The bottom of the dock is coated in a thick, slimy layer of algae, and it smells like my sister's diaper pail. With my ears submerged, I can't hear whether the dogs have reached the lakeside. I can only hear my heartbeat. I stay there for what feels like an eternity until it gets too dark to see and the skin on my fingers becomes tight and wrinkly. When I finally emerge, bone-tired from treading water, I flop onto the bank. Fireflies bob in the air above me, their bioluminescent glow throwing frightening shadows upon the trunks of trees.

"Dad?" I shout. "Father Ricci?" While my voice echoes, no one answers. When I return to the church hours later, shivering and damp, they barely look up from their card game.

Wharton, Virginia—Present Day

I find shelter in a small hunting blind three miles outside of Wharton proper. Whoever camped here last season left a few supplies: a half-roll of toilet paper, a bottle of bug spray with only a tiny amount of fluid inside, and a flashlight that flickers violently when I switch it on. I squat inside the blind, not wanting to sit on the cold ground. It'll sap all the heat from my body, and I'll be shivering within minutes. I shove wads of toilet paper into my boots, hoping it'll provide enough insulation to keep my feet warm.

My gun, stuffed into my waistband, butts uncomfortably against my hipbone. Failure sits heavily upon my back, driving my heels into the ground. I've been shooting for decades. How could I have missed from only twelve yards away? "Stupid," I grumble, driving a fist into the wall of the blind. The whole structure shakes, threatening to topple down on top of me. "Stupid, stupid, stupid!"

When the sun goes down, I curl up on the ground, my hands tucked inside the sleeves of my jacket. It's blisteringly cold, and I worry that I won't wake up come morning. I'm not foolish enough to backtrack to my car or the hotel. Cordelia will have told them everything. I don't want to wake up to a beast's stinking breath on my face. With my head pillowed on my arm, I stare out the mesh window at the dark forest. The tree branches sway in the breeze, inky black against the gray, moonlit sky. I stare so long that the branches start to look like bony hands, beckoning to me.

I dream of my father. He screams at me, his spittle flecking my cheeks. But I can't quite hear him. It's as though my ears are stuffed with cotton, his voice only registering as distant thunder. The vein in his temple pulses in time with his heartbeat. We're standing in his office in the home we shared in Tennessee. It looks smaller than I remember. The wood-paneled walls seem to breathe, pressing in on us. The taxidermied heads, once terrifying, look pathetic. Something—perhaps a rat—chewed holes in the moose's drooping ears, revealing the wire frame beneath. Its fur is sun-bleached, a whole patch missing on its cheek.

My father grabs me by my shoulders, shaking me. His fingers hook into the divot beneath my clavicle. He's still shouting, but I don't need to hear him to catch his meaning. It's the same refrain to the same tiresome song: you're a failure, an embarrassment, a mistake.

"Then why am I the one who has to hold the gun?" I ask him. "Why does it have to be me?"

I wake to a nuthatch tittering just outside of the blind. "Ha, ha!" it trumpets. It feels poetic to be laughed at. I kick the side of the blind to shoo it away, and it flutters to a faraway branch. I can still dimly hear its song: "Ha-ha, ha! Ha! Ha!"

While I can see my breath, I can still feel—and wiggle—all of my extremities. There's something comforting about waking up outdoors, sucking in clean air and listening to birdsong first thing. Crawling out of the blind, I stand and stretch, bending over to touch my toes. The nuthatch returns. It hops from branch to branch, looking at me through unreadable, black eyes. I search my jacket and pant pockets for a tiny morsel to offer it, finding a few crumbs that I think may have once been a Nature Valley granola bar.

I cup the small pile of crumbs in my palm, holding it out to the tiny bird. It hops closer, its gray wings tucked tight against its pudgy body. "Ha-ha?" it asks.

After several minutes, the bird decides I'm not a threat. It alights on my hand, dipping its head to sample the tidbits of granola. It is lighter than I expect. Before it can fly away, I trap it between my hands. It never laughs again.

CHAPTER 18
(ANGUS)

---◁◆▷---

The chapel at Wharton Med is simple: three rows of cramped pews topped with velvet cushions, facing a nondescript altar covered in votive candles. Neither a cross nor crucifix adorns the reredos because the chapel is meant to be a comfort to all who may enter, regardless of ideology. Only a few candles are lit, representing patients who need a prayer or a light to guide them home. I'm not a religious man, but there's something comforting about the candles. Perhaps it's a vestigial itch. After all, fire kept our Cro-Magnon ancestors safe from predators and cooked disease out of their food.

I light a candle for Hunter and sit in the first pew. When the heater near the altar kicks on, the flame trembles, threatening to extinguish itself in the pool of wax. Resting my elbows on my knees, I stare at it until my eyes blur, damp with unshed tears. Hope, which once roosted in my chest, has flown away. There's only an empty nest now, stuffed full of dry moss and curlicues of bark that can catch fire. "C'mon, Hunter," I mutter through gritted teeth.

"Angus?" Candy leans into the chapel, a greasy Dottie's Diner bag in-hand. "You need to eat." Without waiting for an invitation, she comes to sit beside me, dropping the bag on the pew between us. The scent of French fries, flash-fried in peanut oil, makes my stomach roil.

"I'm not hungry." Hunter's candle burns brightly now. I sit back, watching the smoke drift skyward. The ceiling just above the altar is black with soot. "Have you eaten?" I ask her.

Candace Bailey and I have spent more time together in the last week than we have in the previous eighteen months. I find her presence comforting. She often does very Hunter-like things without realizing it, like clicking her tongue when deep in thought. Often, we both fall asleep on the futon in Hunter's hospital room, laying head to foot.

"No," Candy admits, her shoulders drooping. "It all just tastes like ash."

I know what she means. Food has lost all flavor. Each bite seems to swell in my mouth as I chew, threatening to clog my airway when it is time to swallow. It sits in my stomach like a lead weight. I haven't eaten in days, subsisting off of lukewarm coffee from the machine. I like to go upstairs to the labor and delivery ward to get it so that I can touch the doorknob of the janitor's closet where I last kissed him.

"He's looking better," she says, abruptly changing the subject. "His cheeks are pinking up."

"I think," I murmur, keenly aware of the hard lump in my throat. "I think he's going to die." The votive's flame bobs, dimming to an ember as if taunting me. I press the heels of my hands into my eye sockets. "He's too fragile, Candace. If we try to take him off the ventilator again, his heart could just … stop."

"Angus." Candy rests her hand on my shoulder. "There's still hope—there has to be."

I shrug her off, rising to pace the length of the room. "All I can think about is how none of this would have happened if I had chosen anywhere else in the world to run to. Why did I come to Wharton?" If I hadn't retreated to my Granny's bosom like a pup, Hunter wouldn't know the bite of a bullet—or teeth.

Candy watches me pace. She fiddles with the sleeve of her cardigan, the hem raw and unraveled. It looks as though it has been chewed up by a dog. "Do you really think Hunter wishes you never came?"

"I think he wouldn't know pain like this," I admit. My voice cracks. I turn away from her, shoving my fists into my pockets. I stare at the votives until my vision blurs.

"You're feeling sorry for yourself," Candy observes coolly. "I get it. But how is that helping my brother?"

"I can't help him," I snap, agitated. "I'm just spinning my wheels here." Sitting at his bedside has shown me how very little power I have.

"Can't you?" Candy counters. She rises, so that we are eye-to-eye. Or rather, eye-to-mouth. She is a hair shorter than her brother. "Stop gatekeeping. He's already in your world—give him what he fucking wants."

✦ ✦ ✦

A nurse comes in to check Hunter's vitals every two hours. I let Haley Campbell into his room five minutes after midnight, knowing we'll have privacy until two o'clock. I lean back against the door. The room is dark, lit only by the various machines keeping Hunter alive. The green glow of the heartrate monitor makes his skin appear sickly. I flip the switch for the light above the headboard. "You're sure no one will come in?" Haley asks.

"Not for hours," I lie. The truth is, as soon as his heart rate decelerates and the alarm sounds, the nursing staff will call a code. They'll come barreling down the hall with a crash cart, paddles at the ready. But we can't wait any longer. Every passing second feels like borrowed time.

Haley rubs her dry hands together. "Are you sure about this?"

"Just get on with it," I bark, shuffling over to Hunter's bedside to grip his hand.

Haley gently folds back Hunter's blanket so she can reach his other arm. She lifts it by the wrist, turning it palm up. She parts her lips, revealing a row of crowded incisors bookended by keen fangs. "I'll be gentle," she assures me. Or rather, I think that's what she says. It sounds as though she has marbles in her mouth.

She sinks her teeth into the fleshy muscle on his forearm, just below the crease of his elbow. Blood soaks the sheets. Haley's fingers dimple the flesh of Hunter's wrist and bicep as she takes another bite. The heart rate monitor climbs from 60 to 100 beats per minute. "Haley," I growl. "Let go of him."

"He tastes so ... good," she moans. "Just one more little ... nibble."

I reach across the bed, grabbing the she-wolf by the throat. "Let ... go!" I command, giving her a furious shake. Haley snarls at me, but she retreats, using the edge of her finger to wipe the blood coating her chin into her greedy mouth. Her eyes are black pools. "Snap out of it. Remember, you're doing this for Candy."

Haley blinks, and her pupils contract back to their normal size. She wipes her blood-slick hands on her jeans in disgust, "Oh God," she whimpers, spitting blood onto the linoleum. "I didn't hurt him, did I?"

His arm is flayed open, a bit of fibrous muscle visible beneath the skin. But the bleeding has already slowed to an ooze. The heart rate monitor falls to 75. "No," I say, relief flooding my body. "I think it's healing."

Suddenly, Hunter's green eyes open. At first, I think it is a fluke. He's opened them before. The sedatives make him too sleepy to remain awake, but they don't stop him from waking for a minute or two at a time. But then, he flails, hooking his fingers around the strap keeping the ventilator in place. "Hunter! Hunter!" I try to grasp his hands. "Hunter, can you hear me?"

Hunter rips the nasogastric tube from out of his nostril, gnashing his teeth against the thick endotracheal tube. A gargling moan escapes him, and he grasps the endotracheal tube with both hands, pulling it out inch by inch. The cuff meant to keep the tube secure in his airway is still inflated and soaked with saliva.

Abruptly, he sits up, pushing me away. He throws his sock-clad feet over the side of the bed, using the handrail to pull himself upright. His hospital gown flutters, revealing the length of his back and his pert butt. There's a patch of inflammation on one cheek, the early stages of bedsore.

"Hunter—" I reach for his hand, but he side-steps away from me. The electrodes, still attached to his hairless chest, pop off. The heart rate monitor's screen reads NO SIGNAL and an alarm keens. I hurriedly turn the machine off, not wanting a nurse to come investigate. "You need to sit down, c'mon let's—"

Hunter stumbles, falling to his knees. The crack of his kneecaps on the cold linoleum sounds like a pool stick striking a cue ball. I wince, but Hunter doesn't cry out, even though the pain must be immeasurable. He scurries along the floor on his hands and the balls of his feet, heading toward the door. Haley jumps out of his way, her face pale. I don't blame her. I feel a bit queasy myself. We were born wolfish. Those two parts of ourselves are not unlike twins, holding hands in the womb. Conversely, Hunter and the wolf are strangers, both vying for control of one body.

Hunter scrambles to his feet, his palms walking up the door. Then, without ceremony, he slams his face into the rectangle of glass that looks out onto the empty hall. "Oh, what the fuck," Haley moans. A hairline fracture webs the glass, but it doesn't break. Blood streams from his nose, wet droplets peppering the linoleum.

Hunter's flapping hands find the handle, pushing the door open. Without so much as a glance, he shuffles down the hall, his bare ass hanging out of his gown "What do we do?" Haley asks, wringing her hands. I'm already speed-walking after him. Hunter walks with purpose, his blood-crusted nostrils flaring. I am a little afraid to touch him, thinking of sleepwalkers who wake so frightened that they run into oncoming traffic. Though, Hunter isn't asleep, is he?

Hunter plods through the labyrinthine corridors of the ICU. The unit is laid out like the spokes of a wheel, the atrium housing the nurse's station acting as the axle. He has the sense to stay out of sight of the nurse's station, though we are near enough that I can overhear their conversation. Dr. Fitzsimmons is apparently sleeping with one of the interns.

Outside one of the myriad patient rooms, Hunter pauses. His breath fogs the glass. I imagine the velociraptor in *Jurassic Park*.

"Hunter?" I murmur, tentatively touching his arm. His skin is hot and moist, his body wracked with fever.

Through the rectangular window, I catch a glimpse of a room the mirror image of his own. The occupant is asleep, his leg encased in a fiberglass cast from ankle to hip, propped up on a pile of pillows. A square of gauze is taped to his cheek, the fabric stained red with blood. Even with the door closed, I can smell it: cloying and coppery. Hunter can too.

Hunter murmurs something under his breath, his hand alighting on the door handle. "No, no, no," I hiss, grabbing his wrist. "Hunter, Hunter! Look at me."

His green eyes seem to look through me. But his shoulders slump, and he continues his shuffling totter down the hall. "Hungry," he garbles.

"Hunter!" This time, when I touch his arm, he whirls. His hospital gown flares outward like a cape. He bares his squarish teeth at me then breaks into a sprint. I run after him, nearly vaulting over a wheelchair left in the corridor. He is much more nimble than a barefooted man has any right to be, and soon, I lose him amidst the maze of hallways. I peer into every room I pass, terrified that I will find him crouched like a gargoyle upon someone's bed.

The hall terminates at an elevator, a bit of blood on the button. I can dimly hear the whirring of the motor inside. The cab is in motion. I curse under my breath, punching the button to call the elevator back. But I can only watch helplessly as the screen counts down from three to one.

CHAPTER 19
(HUNTER)

————◁◆▷————

I wake on the sand, the locomotive roar of the ocean a dull ache in my inner ear. Stratus clouds lay thickly atop the troposphere; it's as though the planet— or, at least, my tiny corner of it—is covered in a goose- down comforter. The sun can't breach the blanket of clouds, giving Tranquil Cove a sort of dreary ambi- ance. Seagulls wheel beneath the cloud cover, dipping down to inspect me. Perhaps I look like an overly large mussel. I feel like one: a lump with a hard exterior, doomed to scoot across the substrate whilst larger creatures circle overhead.

I get to my feet. Tranquil Cove is no longer an inlet, but an expanse of satiny, water-logged sand. My feet don't leave footprints. Instead, fluidized sand sluices into the shallow indentation until it looks undisturbed. It feels unnerving to look back and see no evidence of my progress; perhaps I don't exist at all.

Rocky tidepools dot the landscape, inhabited by sea stars, crabs, urchins, and small bullet-shaped fish. I kneel beside a pool populated by a colony of *hermit crabs, resting my elbows on my knees. A small crab with a blue shell catches my attention. On closer inspection, the hermit crab's shell is painted, the color chipped away here and there to reveal the mottled, caramel-colored shell underneath. A comma-shaped smudge of gray and red adorns the whorl of its shell. It's unreadable now, but I know what it once was: the New England Patriots logo. "Tommy?" I ask the crab as it flexes its claws. "Is that you, buddy?" As a kid, I rescued the crab from a stinky cage at Sun 'n Stuff, gave it the name of my favorite Power Ranger, and let it free on the beach behind the shop. I thought for certain he would be gobbled up by a seagull, but it was better than being in a cage.*

"We can't keep meeting like this," a familiar voice says.

I whirl around to find Leigh Volkov, her dark hair braided over her shoulder. She hooks her thumbs in the pockets of her cutoffs, her eyes half-lidded as though I'm already boring her. I am relieved to see that she's entirely whole, with not so much as a scraped knee, let alone a shattered clavicle. She's wearing the same outfit she wore when we met: cutoffs, an oversized men's button-down that hangs off of her narrow shoulders, and aviator sunglasses perched upon her brow. "Why do I keep seeing you everywhere?" I ask.

"You keep trying to die." Leigh shrugs her shoulders as if to say, Don't think too hard about it. She sidles closer, kicking at the sand with the scuffed toe of her Converse high-top. The laces are untied, the aglets frayed.

"But why you?"

"Does it matter?" she counters, tipping her head so that the sunglasses fall onto the bridge of her nose. I can see my reflection in the lenses. It is only then that I realize I'm wearing a three-piece suit, my hair slicked back flat against my scalp. "You don't have a lot of time left," she adds.

"I look like I'm going to a wedding." There's a boutonniere pinned to my lapel. A blue daffodil rests amidst a handful of cup-shaped waxflowers and a sprig of baby's breath. Blue makes me yearn for Angus. I want to look into his eyes, even for just a moment. If I had known the last time—freezing in that ditch, my head cradled in his lap—was truly the last time, I would have savored it. I wouldn't have prayed so hard to die.

"Or a funeral." Leigh kneels beside the tidepool, plunging her hand into the water. The crabs scatter. "Though, judging by your sister, your family seems like the type to bury you in a Hawaiian shirt because it's more fun." Leigh scoops up a hermit crab. I catch a glimpse of its blue shell before she traps it between her cupped hands. "You can hear them, can't you? They're talking about you—what to do. It's all very dour."

"Who?" I find myself staring at her hands, at the hermit crab's bristly legs poking between her fingers. It is testing her grip, searching for a way back to its home. It didn't survive that Sun 'n Stuff cage, subsisting off a meager diet of fish meal flakes, just to succumb to a human's whims.

Leigh's lip twitches. "Gus. Your sister, too. You really haven't been listening?" She drops the hermit crab back into the pool. Plop! I catch only the briefest glimpse of the smudged Pats logo on its nautilus-shaped shell before the crab scurries beneath a bit of kelp. Relief floods my body. I had half-expected her to pry him from his shell and snap each of his legs off. "Or maybe you just like being here."

"Where's here?"

Leigh flicks me smack dab between my eyes. "In your head." She grins widely, revealing canine teeth that are just a smidge too sharp.

I scoff, rubbing at my forehead. "I doubt that, of all of the people in the world I could conjure up, I'd choose you."

Leigh stretches, grasping her elbow with the opposite hand to manipulate the tricep. For a moment, the fingertips of her right hand alight upon her left shoulder. Before I can tell her to stop, the elbow joint snaps. The arm goes floppy, held together only by muscle, flesh, and my mumbled prayer ("Oh God, oh God, no, no, not again"). I turn away from her, my hands on my knees. "You're the one torturing yourself, Hunter," Leigh says. "Right now? This is all you."

I'm certain that I'm going to be sick. I stumble away from the tidepool, not wanting to catch a whiff of brine or algae. I breathe through my mouth, but then I think that I can taste the pool's contents. I retch, a tendril of saliva clinging to my lip.

"Don't get me wrong," Leigh continues, unfazed by my outburst. "I'm certainly not happy that I'm dead. I'm pissed, actually. I had a lot of fun things planned for your boyfriend that I never got to do. But I'm not haunting you."

Slowly, the wave of nausea abates. I shoot the woman a furtive glance. Her arms are crossed over her chest now, all of the bones seemingly repaired. "You said Angus and Candy ... they were talking about me?"

"They spend all of their time talking about you. They sit at your bedside for hours, talking and talking. They have the same conversation, a hundred different ways. It always ends the same: you're dying, and there's nothing they can do, except—" She pauses, tapping at her chin with her acrylic nail. "—tonight, I think they're done talking."

I wish my subconscious' version of Leigh wouldn't talk in circles. If only her words were riddles; there might be some logic imbued in them, then.

"This is going to hurt, Hunter," she says. "You're going to wish you had died. Maybe, it'll hurt so much you'll throw yourself in front of a car to escape it. Wouldn't that be ironic? I think that would make me rest peacefully, wherever your boyfriend buried me."

I'm tired of listening to her. I move to walk past her, but she sticks her foot out, tripping me. I fall into the cold tidepool, my chin colliding with an algae-slick rock. Stars burst in front of my eyes, multiplying until all I see is—

—the light above my bed.

I wake on a strange planet, surrounded by noisy machinery. One beeps intermittently, its screen transmitting neon-colored glyphs that I can't readily decipher: HR, SpO2, RR. Another clicks and wheezes, its rhythm coinciding with an unsettling fullness in my chest. I am aware of two figures at my bedside, their forms blurry and indistinct. One speaks, but its voice is not unlike the "wah wah wah" of Charlie Brown's teacher.

My stomach cramps. It feels like a fist driven into my abdomen. That's what woke me from my cryosleep, I think: I'm ravenously hungry. I find myself thinking of the sirloin at Dottie's Diner, swimming in myoglobin and butter, topped with a sprig of thyme. *God.* If I hurry, perhaps I can get to the restaurant before it closes. Surely, this planet has a Dottie's.

Hun ... gry.

Starving! The thought is my own but seems to come from a more persistent voice inside my head. It was as though I felt a draft and woke up to a cat burglar climbing in through the window. Now, the cat burglar has his dirty feet up on my hippocampus, asking to be served hors d'oeuvres.

Click. There's the pressure in my chest again. My lungs inflate like party balloons, just beyond the point of comfort. *Hissss.* Before they can pop, the pressure abates. I'm suffocating. But before I can thrash, the machine clicks, and air pours into my chest cavity again. The machine is breathing for me. I grasp the tube snaking into my nostril, giving it a sharp tug. It feels like removing a particularly stubborn booger, rooted in my sinus cavity. The figure closest to my bedside lets out a startled bleat. I grasp the tube wedged between my jaws with both hands, pulling with all of my might. Something hard and unyielding scrapes against my soft palate, making me gag. Still, I pull hand over hand, desperate to get out of this bed. Finally, the bulbous end of the tube clears my throat and I toss it aside. My throat feels as though it's lined with gritty sandpaper. I sit up, swinging my legs over the side of the bed.

Hungry, the voice insists.

The room smells of antiseptic and a little like body odor, though I think the latter might be me. I've been asleep for a millennia, after all. I slowly stand, finding my legs as wobbly as a newborn foal's. I sway a bit, but I don't tumble over.

"Hunter—" One of the figures reaches out to me, but I avoid its touch. How does it know my name? It feels like a trick; it'll offer me comfort and then—snap!—it'll swallow me whole like a Venus flytrap. "You need to sit down, c'mon..."

I move too quickly to get away from the figure, falling onto my knees. My gown pools around me, two blotches of red blooming on the fabric. My knees are bleeding. I expect to feel pain, but there is very little. It cannot compete with the burning acid chewing up the walls of my stomach. *God, I'm so...*

"Hunter!"

I need to get out of here. There's a door. I scurry across the floor on hands and feet, and the second figure screams. Perhaps I look like a rat. It's an apt comparison. I am certain that I would dig through a stinking dumpster if I was promised a crumb. I press my palms against the door, looking through the window at the hall.

My stomach burbles.

I bash my head into the glass. As with my knees, the pain hardly registers. It is a means to an end. A spiderweb of hairline fractures spread across the pane. I almost don't recognize my reflection in the fissured glass. I look small and rail thin, my knobby shoulder peeking out of the untied gown. My facial hair is unkempt, the wispy hairs of my mustache tickling my lip. I look ghoulish.

We're hungry, the voice reminds me. *Go. Run. EAT!*

I look back. My breath catches, and for just a moment, I wish for the mechanical inhale offered by the machine. The figures are wearing the faces of Angus and Haley. Surely, it's a hologram—I can see two of Angus, the twin images pulling apart like a cell in mitosis. "Hunter," he murmurs, reaching for me with two—*four*—arms.

Blood drips down my nose, but I don't understand that I may have given myself a concussion. Fear trumps logic. I need to get out of here, at any cost.

I manage to engage the doorknob, though my hands feel as though they belong to someone else. I am aware of the not-Angus talking to me, but I don't acknowledge him. Perhaps if I ignore him, he will go away. No more than three steps into the hall, I am aware of the scent of blood. It makes my stomach gurgle. Before I can investigate, the not-Angus stops me.

I wish he would leave me alone. When I run, my bare feet slapping against the cool linoleum, I am certain that I have never been so free.

CHAPTER 20
(HENRY)

—◁◆▷—

Sevierville, Tennessee—August 1970

The stained-glass flanking the nave of St. Cyprian's casts a lurid, varicolored glow upon the pulpit. The trio of lancet windows depicts Adam and Eve's expulsion from the Garden of Eden.

On the left side of the pulpit, Eve consorts with the serpent, its scaly coils wrapped around her comely legs. She is nude, her nipples and hairless pubis tinted pink. Father Ricci says that it is not meant to be scandalous. In that moment, Eve is as innocent as a newborn babe. Still, I try not to look at her during mass because the image makes my own serpent stir.

Behind the pulpit, Adam and Eve are depicted with eyes as wide as saucers, the half-eaten apple forgotten on the ground. They cover their nudity with splayed hands. In most churches, the wall beyond the chancel arch is windowless, reserved for a crucifix or perhaps a large tapestry. But at St. Cyprian's, the congregants at morning mass must look directly into the rising sun. I am fairly certain that the red of the bitten apple is tattooed onto my retinas.

The third lance-shaped window depicts a more pastoral scene. The garden gates are flung open, revealing a cuddling lion and lamb draped in floral garlands. A disembodied hand shoos the two sinners into the desert, now clothed in drab, sand-colored robes.

As Samuel drags me through the nave by my shirt collar, voices float up from the basement. When we reach the top of the stairs, Samuel releases me. His jaw works as though he's chewing gum. I wonder if he's working out what he's going to say when he confronts my father and the priest. "Stay here, Henry," he commands gruffly before heading down the stairwell, the bent rifle resting upon his shoulder.

I shift from foot to foot. The stained glass throws color on the floor, the red of the apple resembling spilt Kool-Aid on the brown carpet. The nave is empty, but somewhere in the rafters, I can hear fluttering. Sometimes, pigeons get in when the doors are left open, roosting atop the heavy beams that crisscross the ceiling. Father Ricci ushers them out with a broom, but they always return. It's become a rule to check one's pew before sitting; it's difficult to get greasy white bird shit out of church slacks or nylon dresses.

Abruptly, the raucous chatter stops. I stick my finger in my ear, giving it a little swirl. Have I gone deaf? Then, the screams start. Before I can think better of it, I fly down the stairs, my palm skimming the rail.

The pews in the basement have been pushed against the walls, making room for a card table and chairs. Erotic playing cards litter the tabletop; they'd been in the middle of a game when Samuel interrupted. A cigar smolders atop the ten of diamonds, a hand's length from the glass ashtray. A pinup wearing a war bonnet, garters, and little else poses on the face. Just as I skitter into the room, Samuel shoves the table aside.

"You send a child to kill me?" he snarls. His body seems to swell, the seams of his shirtsleeves popping.

"Saint Michael!" Father Ricci shouts. "The Archangel! Defend us in battle!"

Samuel's shirt falls around his waist in ribbons, the muscles of his back bulging. His skin rolls as if there are thousands of beetles skittering just beneath it. "Battle?" he snickers. His voice sounds like crushed glass underfoot.

My father climbs over the pews, desperate to get away from my stepfather. He tries to open the hopper windows, but they hardly budge; I think they've been nailed shut, to prevent teenagers from breaking into the church basement to cavort and canoodle. Only the church elders are allowed to enjoy those sinful things, judging by the cards, cigars, and the bottle of Canadian Club resting on the pew.

Samuel's scapula snaps, pulling his left shoulder up to his earlobe. Fur bursts from his pores, cascading down his back. "What's the matter, Milton?" he taunts. "Are you frightened?"

My father tries to pry the nails out of the window frames with his fingers. He's like a rat in a sinking ship, searching for something—anything—to float upon. His fingertips bleed.

Samuel turns his head to look at me through one dark eye. His lips pull away from his teeth in what I imagine is a smile. "Don't you see? He's a coward. He sent you to do his bidding because he doesn't care about you."

My father missteps, tumbling off the pew. The air jettisons from his lungs, the sound not unlike a party balloon when you pinch the neck. If I wasn't so frightened, I would laugh. He gulps for air, his face tomato red.

Father Ricci reaches into his cassock, pulling out the pistol he'd used to teach me to shoot all those weeks ago. Pulling back the hammer, his hand steady, he aims at the beast's head. He's still praying to the Archangel Michael. "May God rebuke him, we humbly pray!" The handgun looks puny compared to the enormous wolf-man. Surely, a bullet would only be an annoyance, like a buzzing mosquito in summertime. Father Ricci should ask the angel for his flaming sword instead.

Samuel lunges at the priest, grabbing him by the throat. Father Ricci's clerical collar comes loose, fluttering to the ground. The gun goes off, the bullet plunging into the drywall just inches from my head. I duck, clamping my palms over my ears. But, it's too late; the sound ping-pongs between my eardrums, usurping all other noise. I can't hear what Father Ricci is screaming, though I can see the spittle flying off of his tongue.

The priest's mouth stills, his tongue folding back against his soft palate. Angry patches of red erupt on his cheeks. His eyes bulge, so much so that I expect them to just pop out of the sockets like a cartoon character in love. Clawing at the beast's hairy arm, his movements become sluggish. Slowly, the ringing in my ears ebbs, and I can hear the wet whistling escaping his nostrils. Each time he tries to suck in a breath, Samuel squeezes just a little bit harder. I can't help but think of the portrait of the Kayan woman in my history textbook, her neck made long and narrow by brass coils. If Samuel releases the priest, I imagine his neck will fold over, unable to support the weight of his skull.

My father rises unsteadily, grabbing the bottle of Canadian Club by the neck. The whisky sloshes, a bit of froth clinging to the glass. He swings it at the wolf-man, striking him just between the ears. Samuel snarls, tossing the priest aside like a ragdoll. He crashes into the card table, the flimsy legs buckling under his weight. I think he may be dead. Fingertip bruises are dark against his sallow skin, and petechiae dots his cheeks like freckles. He stares at the ceiling, his sclera gone purple.

Samuel grabs my father by the hair, bashing his forehead into the pew. The wet crack, not unlike a watermelon on pavement, turns my stomach. I stumble toward the baptismal font to steady myself, my foot colliding with something cold and metallic on the floor. It's Father Ricci's revolver. I bend to pick it up.

Samuel lifts his arm high to slam my father's skull into the pew again, "Stop!" I shout, tugging at the wolf-man's fur. "Dad, stop!"

Samuel freezes. It's the first time I've ever called him dad. He's always just been Samuel because I have a father. It was bad luck that I got a cruel and cold one in Milton Fairbanks. It could be worse. My pal Eddie has no father at all—he went out for a pack of Newports when Eddie was in kindergarten and never came back.

"What did you say?" the wolf asks.

My father dangles by his hair from Samuel's fist, his toes barely skidding upon the carpet. Blood trickles down his hairline, the skin of his forehead pulled taut as though he's had a facelift. He paws weakly at Samuel's fist, trying to take pressure off of his scalp. Strands of hair snap at the midsection, the remaining baby hair curling. There's a wet patch on his slacks; he's pissed himself. He looks at me with round eyes, mouthing words I can't decipher.

"Please," I say, "put him down."

Samuel releases my father, who falls into a heap at my feet. "You called me 'dad,'" he murmurs.

I look down at my father. Milton swipes at his forehead, smearing blood. The viscous liquid mixes with his tears, turning pink and watery. He pulls his knees to his chest, as though wanting to disappear. With his long limbs and great height, it just makes him look silly. He looks up at me, his lower lip quivering. I've never seen him cry before. "Henry Lee," he blubbers, "Honor thy father, or be stoned with stones." He's mixed up Ephesians and Deuteronomy, but that's not his fault. Surely, he has a concussion.

The gun is so heavy that it pulls down my shoulder. "I know, dad," I say soothingly.

Samuel's eyes settle on the gun. "Are you going to shoot me, Henry?"

"Are you the devil?" I ask, pulling down the hammer with my thumb. It's a big stretch for my child-sized hand, and the adductor muscle in my palm cramps painfully. I switch the gun from my right to my left hand.

"No," Samuel says. "I'm just a man."

I scoff. If he's just a man, I'm a teapot. "You're a monster, like in that movie with the manor house and the scientist." My mother and I went to go see the rerelease of *Don't Look in the Lake!* at the Filmland Theater, sharing a paper bag of buttery popcorn. With a pang, I remember how cruel I was afterward. *Why did you pick this one? You said it'd be scary, but there was kissing!* Mom was quiet on the drive home. Would it have been so hard to just say, "Mom, I had a good time with you?" Whatever happens here, I know that I will never be able to see her again. Not for a long time, anyway.

I glance at the crumpled body of the priest. There's a bloodless divot in his bald head, from where his skull collided with the floor. "You killed Father Ricci."

"I did. He was dangerous. He's been filling your father's head with lies. Yours too." The wolf sits on his haunches, curling his tail around his paws.

"He was a holy man," I counter. "He was my —" I press my lips together, too embarrassed to continue. I don't want to tell him that sometimes, when my father is particularly drunk, the skunk-smell seeping through the vents, I pretend Father Ricci is my dad.

The wolf hacks. I can't tell if it's a cough or a chuckle. He looks pointedly at the overturned card table. "Oh yes, very holy. Very righteous."

My father sits up, pressing the heel of his hand against his bleeding scalp. "Henry Lee," he pants. "Do … your … duty. The devil is trying to get in your head, boy! Shoot him!"

Wharton, Virginia—Present Day

The nuthatch tastes gamey, the meat charred and dry. Still, I swallow every morsel, licking at my greasy fingers between bites. I managed to light a small, dwindling fire, using the wadded-up toilet paper as tinder. The smoke clings to my clothes and hair. A neat pile of bones, feathers, and inedible innards sits beside the fire, throwing grotesquely misshapen shadows across the clearing.

For a moment, I contemplate packing my things and leaving town. I've squandered what higher ground I had. Surely, the beasts and their allies have circled the proverbial wagons. Who will know of my failure if I just go? My loudest critic is in my own head, speaking exclusively in my father's critical tone.

Failure.

I pop the last bit of meat into my mouth, a sliver of bone crunching between my molars. Perhaps I haven't failed after all. I've only been biding my time. Evil always falters. Even Lucifer fell from On High. *Yes, that's it.* I waited, oh so fucking patiently, and Samuel Campbell died, withered and miserable. I waited, and our family line was whittled down into a splinter, easily excised. The Lord works in mysterious ways, so perhaps the missed shot on Bird's Nest was a godsend. I feel badly that I hurt someone, but martyrs must be made. What was it that my mother used to say about eggs? You can't make a cake without breaking some.

I pick up Samuel's diary. It is misshapen from roosting inside my jacket, nearly bent in half. Some of the pages have come loose from the binding, and when I open it, they fall onto my lap. The sheet on top is from the middle of an entry and starts mid-sentence.

> *...him to Wharton. Ama says he looks like me, which is funny considering who his daddy is. But he's my boy, and I love him more than I could ever fathom I would. Maybe that rubs off on a person, even if you aren't blood. Maybe there's an invisible mark that only Ama sees, cause she's a perceptive broad. I swear that woman is made of different stuff than the rest of us.*

The name conjures a memory of a cluttered porch, an icy glass of lemonade pressed against my neck, and a euphonious laugh. We stayed at their house when we visited, camping in the living room atop a pile of sleeping bags. Her daughter was the same age as Cordy — maybe younger — and her face turned purple when I snatched a frisbee out of her hands. "Henry," Ama admonished me, "we cannot take toys from our friends." The use of "we" always struck me as odd. We didn't do it. *I* did. It was as though she wanted to shoulder the blame so that it didn't feel so heavy. She could tell I was already carrying far more than a child should. If she weren't Samuel's friend, I would have mistook her for a saint.

Surely, she will know where my niece is. Perhaps she's even harboring my wretched sister. With a plan in place, I kick dirt onto the fire, extinguishing it. I tuck the gun into my jacket pocket, giving it a loving pat. It's time to do my duty. If only my father could see it.

CHAPTER 21
(HUNTER)

———◁◆▷———

The "B" on the elevator's control panel lights up when pressed. It is so bright that I turn away, throwing my arm up over my face. A rivulet of blood, now dry and flaky, snakes from my inner elbow to my wrist. A bit of Tegaderm still sticks to my skin; it had been holding an I.V. in place before I unceremoniously ripped it out.

The elevator's cubicle makes me feel claustrophobic, and I pace from corner to corner. I don't know where I'm going, only that every synapse is saying *go*. I am certain that if I don't eat soon, I will die. My stomach is a knot, the ends pulled taut. "Hunger is the great equalizer," I mumble, trying to remember where I'd heard the words before.

The elevator jitters beneath my bare feet. With each passing floor—announced by an irritating *ding* that makes my eyeballs pulse—I become more conscious of my body. I can't take a deep breath; instead, I must take tiny sips of the air. Layers of tightly wrapped bandages compress my chest wall. If I unwrap it, will

I crumble like a dried-up mummy? There is pain too—a deep-set burning just beneath the sternum. I curl around the sunspot of agony, pressing my palms against the flat bone as though it'll douse the blaze.

I sway unsteadily, staring at a flier taped to the wall. "Grief support group," I read aloud. My voice rasps, as though the words were siphoned through a cheese grater before bouncing off of my tongue. A stock photo of a weeping woman accompanies the advertisement, the Shutterstock watermark still transecting the image. Rocking back on my heels, I peer into the woman's eyes. They are brimming with unshed tears, just on the precipice of streaming down her freckled cheeks. She presses her thin lips together as if to contain a sob, which deepens the wrinkles there. It's a fitting image: grief is like being frozen in one's ugliest moment.

Ding! The doors slide open. The hospital's bowels are gray and industrial, the ductwork visible in the ceiling. It smells like the seafood case in the supermarket. Perhaps this is where they store the food they serve to patients, where they load up those little carts with cloche-covered dishes. I imagine pawing through a freezer case, tearing open the plastic-wrapped foam trays laden with salmon filet and ground beef. The thought of shoving the contents, still frozen, into my mouth fills me with ecstasy.

The exit signs above the nearest double door buzzes; the battery is dying. I approach the doors, finding a placard reading RESTRICTED ACCESS. I tentatively push the doors, expecting an alarm to sound, but none does.

They swing open at my slightest touch, revealing a dim room. On the nearest wall, a whiteboard with the heading "Body Fridge Room Status" lists the number of bodies in cold storage, whether they are claimed or unclaimed, and if they are whole or in parts. Someone wrote "Merry Christmas, nerds!" in the corner along with a crude drawing of a snowman in a top hat, its eyes x's.

The piscine stench is overwhelming here. I shuffle across the room, my fingertips brushing against the stainless-steel table. It's chilly. There's a drain at one end, a bit of red crust clinging to the rim. I don't know what it's for. I feel as though I *should* know, but I'm having trouble thinking. It's as though there's a stereo playing inside my head, the volume oscillating between a whisper and an eardrum-shaking clamor. It is a repeating message, like a numbers station broadcasting coordinates and mission objectives: *go, run, eat!*

One wall is composed of eighteen drawers, each with a handle and a label. Curious, I pull out the nearest drawer, just enough to catch a glimpse of a bit of dark hair and a smooth forehead. While the sight is disturbing, the smell is worse. It makes my stomach clench. Saliva pools in my mouth, but I'm not sure if it's due to desire or disgust. I slam the drawer shut.

I'm in a morgue. I skitter backward until my bare butt collides with the table. I run back into the hall, looking for any other way out. At the end of the corridor — past closets and what looks like a lab, the machines shrouded in plastic covers — I find a large pan door. Perhaps it leads to a loading dock. I press my cheek against the corrugated metal and can hear the wind. *Yes! A way out!* I lean down to grab the handle, giving it a tug. It doesn't budge.

Go, the voice in my head insists.

I grasp the handle with both hands, but the door is immovable. It must be locked. Hot, frustrated tears stream down my cheeks. I think that I would do anything to get out of here, to quiet the hunger pangs.

Suddenly, my knees bend back as if kicked in. Now, *this* is pain. It is not unlike being shot: sharpness followed by a sizzle followed by an unrelenting ache. There is hardly time to wrap my brain around the pain before the next bone snaps. It feels as though I am being unmade—dismantled piece by piece. I imagine popping the limbs off of Candy's Barbie dolls when we were kids. Leigh was right: I wish I was dead. This tsunami of pain will drown me. When the tide pulls back out, I will be no more.

I press my palms against the door, but my hands are not hands anymore. They have ballooned three times their size, each digit topped by a scythe-like claw. The swelling swallows the ring on my right hand, momentarily cutting off circulation to that finger. The skin turns red, then purple. Unable to resist the pressure, the ring pops at the seam, careening across the room with the force of a bullet. Fur bursts from every pore— mousy gray at the fingertips, going pallid at the wrist— accompanied by an unsettling tingling sensation. It's as though I'm standing too close to an electric fence.

Blindsided by the unending pain, I am only somewhat aware of a tugging in my jaw. The mandible loosens, held in place by the loop of the masseter muscle that serves to open and close the mouth. If I shake my head, I am certain my jaw will pendulate. A feeling unlike anything I'd ever felt before floods my system, dulling the pain. Power.

All at once, my sense of smell increases tenfold. The piquant smell of sweat and infection pours into my nostrils. Then, the cloying odor of bleach and antiseptic. A tiny breeze leaks through the door's seam, and I catch a whiff of something far more appealing.

Hungry!

In this body, it is easy to break the door. The door is comprised of three hinged sections that roll up onto an overhead track, much like a garage door. I punch through the middle section with ease, ripping the metal away with my claws. The metal cuts my paw pads. Fresh air pours in.

"Hunter?" The not-Angus approaches slowly, his hands held out in front of him. I hadn't heard the ding of the elevator over the squeal of ripping metal. I wait for his image to flicker or double as it had in the hospital room, but he looks corporeal. Perhaps it's just Angus, and I've been confused.

"Are you real?" I ask.

"Of course I'm real," Angus says. "Hunt, do you know where you are?" He smells different; it's an earthy odor, like freshly tilled soil made damp by the rain. He'd told me once that wolves can recognize each other by their distinctive, terraceous smell. I'd never understood before because, to my human nose, he just smelled like body wash and freshly laundered clothes.

"Hospital."

"Do you know who you are?" Angus tentatively reaches out, his fingertips combing through the fur on my chest. It is strange to tower over him. For the first time, he looks small—fragile. I could snap him in half.

"Yes," I say. "I'm hungry."

Angus chuckles—or is it a sob? "I'm so sorry, Hunter. I'm sorry you had to wake up like this. You must feel so confused—so scared. But you were dying. I … didn't know what else to do. I couldn't lose you."

The breeze that sweeps through the demolished door ruffles my fur. *Run, run, run,* the voice prompts. "Angus," I murmur. "I told you: this is what I want. Now please: run with me."

I've lived in Wharton for my entire life. I learned to walk on the beach, tumbling onto my bottom until my diaper filled with sand. I know every cove and jetty like the back of my hand. My body is sixty percent salt water.

But I've never experienced Wharton quite like this. Even in the pitch-dark, with only a sliver of the waning moon on the horizon, I can see fairly well. What I cannot readily see, I can smell and hear. I catch a whiff of the boardwalk from three hundred yards away. It's a discordant bouquet: the sickly-sticky-sweetness of cotton candy and sugar-coated churros; the funk of unemptied grease traps and porta-johns; the distinctive odor of Coppertone; and the sulfurous stench of rotting seaweed beneath the pier. Though I cannot see them, I can hear the rats skittering, their naked tails and distending bellies dragging across the rough-hewn pier. Above all, I can smell Angus running alongside me, his tongue lolling out of the side of his mouth. His fur looks silvery in the moonlight.

He leads me into the stretch of forest flanking Tranquil Cove. We skirt around the playground, the swings' chains creaking. We pass the picnic area, startling a plump raccoon digging scraps from the trash can. It grips a bit of bread crust in its human-like paws, chattering obscenities. When we finally reach the beach, I expect to see it as it was in my dream: an alien moonscape. But, to my relief, it looks as it always has. Sea foam tickles our paws as we trot along the shoreline. "When I was asleep, this is where I was," I say. "On this beach."

"It's a beautiful place," Angus says. There's relief in his voice. "Could you hear us ... while you were asleep?"

"No," I admit. "But I don't think I was listening. She told me I wasn't."

Angus slows to a stop. In the darkness, his blue eyes look gray, much like the slow-rolling ocean. "Who?"

"Leigh."

Angus' ears lay flat against his skull. "Hunter—" he growls. He expects us to argue, to rehash the same old dispute. But I'm not trying to make him feel guilty.

"When I dreamt of her, she looked just as irritated as you do." I chuckle. Or rather, I try to. It sounds like a sneeze. "She really let me have it."

"I miss her, you know," Angus whimpers. "Despite everything that she did." While he cannot cry in this form, his shoulders shake. "I let her go after James died because I loved her like a sister. Why couldn't she have just stayed gone?" I nuzzle him, inhaling his musky scent. He leans into me for a moment, and I wonder if he is relieved that, now, I am strong enough to hold him upright.

◆ ◆ ◆

Together, we lie amidst the leaf litter; the ground is cold and unyielding. Despite my thick layer of fur, it saps the heat from my belly.

"Look," Angus whispers, pointing his snout toward a copse of trees. There's evidence of human interference here; several of the maples have been reduced to stumps, and others have had their branches excised. There's dried blue spray paint on the trunks left behind. But that's not what Angus is looking at: beyond the coppice, a herd of deer rest. Their shaggy winter coats make them appear unkempt. One of them takes a few steps away from the group, dipping her angular head to sniff at the ground. "Go," Angus urges. "Your body knows what to do."

Go, run, eat!

My back legs are pistons. I breach the cluster of defiled trees within two strides. The deer flee as though they are one entity—crashing together, stepping on each other, their white tails banners of surrender. The doe tries to rejoin the group, but she is several lengths behind them. She lets out a bleat, her pink tongue clenched between squarish teeth. She wheezes.

I close my jaws on her haunch, and she stumbles, her chin smacking against the ground with such incredible force that it bounces. She throws her front legs out, trying to regain her feet, but I'm not letting go. Her hot blood floods my mouth. It soothes my aching throat like hot tea. Her cloven hooves dig furrows in the earth.

Angus is as silent as a specter. He seems to materialize before the struggling doe. He cups her face with the tenderness of a lover, his paws dwarfing her wedge-shaped skull. Then, he gives it a quick twist, breaking her neck. "We don't want her to suffer," he says, dropping her head into the grass. "It's the last kindness we can give her. Now eat."

CHAPTER 22
(ANGUS)

———◁◆▷———

Hunter eats with the gusto of a toddler. He stuffs the steaming meat into his mouth before he's done chewing the previous bite, blood dripping down his chin. His stomach distends. It's been over a week since he's had a real meal, and I worry he'll vomit if he eats much more. Rich, raw venison is far from the "food" sluiced through a nasogastric tube.

"Are you going to have any?" Hunter mumbles around a full mouth. He's found the web of caul fat that clings to the stomach and spleen, and it makes his snout greasy.

"No," I reply. He makes a handsome wolf. His ombré coat is striking. The darkest parts—his snout, toes, and tail—are inky-black, like an overcast night sky. His silvery fur is mottled, ranging from the slate gray of a harbor seal to the dove gray of a river rock. While he's still smaller than I am, his legs are long; he is faster than I am, more nimble. "How are you feeling?"

"Incredible," Hunter says, sitting back on his haunches. Where once there was a gunshot wound, weeping pus, now there is only a whorl of nearly white fur. "It doesn't hurt anymore."

Relief is painful. It flays open the skin, leaving me trembling and breathless. Every emotion I've tamped down because I needed to be strong—for Candy, the pack, my own sake—surges through me. I let out a mournful howl. Hunter rushes to my side, nuzzling my neck, smearing blood and guts on my ivory fur. "I thought you were going to die," I manage, pulling my lips away from my teeth in a grimace. "I really thought—"

"I'm okay," Hunter assures me. "We're okay."

I comb my fingers through the thick ruff of fur at his neck, pulling him close. Our foreheads touch. His breath, slow and even, is hot upon my face. While I could have him now, in this body, I am desperate to feel the peaks and valleys of him that I know. Still, I stroke his stiffening cock amidst the thicket of fur between his muscular thighs, growling into his ear.

When I shrug off my fur, he does too. Together, we tumble onto the grass beside the felled doe, her body emanating a modicum of heat. When he writhes in agony, his bones crunching and shifting, I kiss his tear-sodden cheeks. He is slick with sweat when his body finally stills; coupled with the cold, he violently shivers. Without fur, the cold is bone-deep, but I'm hardly aware of it. I pull Hunter onto my lap, tangling my fingers in his unruly hair. "We're okay," I repeat, kissing his pale lips.

Hunter shivers, but I warm him with my roving hands. His teeth clack against mine as he deepens the kiss, his tongue spilling into my mouth. I can taste the alkaline of the doe's blood on his lips. My cock stiffens, butting up against his thigh. He grips both of our cocks in his hand, stroking them in tandem. I can't take more than a minute of his expert ministrations. I am desperate to cum inside of him. I grasp his butt, pulling him closer. "Hunter—" I breathe, pressing the bulbous head of my cock against his hole. "I missed you so much."

Hunter's nails dig into my back, leaving bloodless furrows. It's a reminder that I don't have to be gentle. We are made of hardier stuff, even in these bodies. With that, I flip him over so that his back is in the grass, his legs coiled around my waist. Hunter pants, his eyes half-lidded. The cold—or is it my touch?—stiffens his pink nipples. I gently touch his face, my calloused thumb gliding along his lower lip. He parts his lips for me, giving my thumb a little suck. I pant as he lasciviously licks and sucks upon my thumb, coating it with saliva. *Flirt.*

I bend forward to kiss him, pressing his thighs into the earth with firm hands. He nips my lip, drawing blood. He sucks my lip between his teeth, making me gasp. What do I taste like? I grind my hips against his ass, making him whimper in longing. He's forgotten about the cold, though his lips are just a bit blue. I will make him sweat. *Oh Hunter, I promise you, I will.* When I press inside of him, he tenses, his spine arching up off the ground.

It is only after I cum that I realize it is snowing.

CHAPTER 23
(HENRY)

————◁◆▷————

Sevierville, Tennessee—August 1970

"Shoot him!" My father, red-faced and sweating, struggles to stand. He grabs onto the pew with both hands, heaving himself upright. The exertion causes blood to pour from the gash on his forehead.

"I ... can't," I say, through trembling lips. It feels as though I'm standing on a shifting tectonic plate. I pray that there truly is an earthquake, and it isn't just my knocking knees, that the church will fold in upon us, and we'll suffocate. *If only.*

"Give me the gun, Henry," Samuel says calmly. I shy away from his sickle-shaped claws. "Son—" The devil speaks in dulcet tones, but that is by design, isn't it? It is an apple dangling on a twisting branch.

Suddenly, my father lunges, grabbing my wrist in his vice-like grip. "You little *fuck*—" he says, but I don't hear the rest. He wrenches my arm, and a sun-spot of pain darkens my vision and deafens my ears.

It feels as though I'm standing at the end of a long tunnel, squinting in a vain attempt to see what is happening at the other end. Is that shadow a man, or an incoming train?

I don't hear the gunshot.

My father stumbles backward, falling on his butt into the pew. Red blooms on his polo, the sodden fabric clinging to his skin. In fits and starts, my hearing returns. A strange burbling sound leaks from his parted lips. A tiny rivulet of blood pours from the corner of his lip.

The gun clatters to the floor. I can't hold onto it with numb fingers. The smell of sulfur fills the room, acrid and rank. The air is hazy. "What ... what happened?" I stutter. My voice sounds far away. I think that I'm in shock. I clutch my broken wrist against my chest.

"We've got to go, Henry," Samuel urges gently. His doggish face seems to melt away, revealing swaths of pale, pinkish skin beneath. His snout dimples, flattening into his angular jaw. He looks around for something to cover his nakedness, finding a chasuble hanging upon a hook. He looks outlandish in the sleeveless vestment, adorned with an embroidered cross, the letters "IHS" traversing the crossbar.

"Why?" I don't understand what has happened. I feel slow, like I'm waist-deep in a vat of molasses. My pal Eddie once told me that molasses flooded a whole town, killing twenty-one people. That story made me laugh—he's such a card. Gosh, my wrist hurts. I turn back to my father. His eyes are wide and unblinking, like he's seen a g-g-g-ghost. "Daddy?" He doesn't answer. Shuffling closer, I reach out and touch his cheek with my uninjured hand. He doesn't flinch. "Dad?"

Samuel grasps my shoulders, tugging me toward the staircase. "Please," he implores. "He's dead, Henry. We have to get out of here."

"I ... don't understand." All I know is that my father broke my wrist. He's thrown things, shaken me by my shoulders, but this has never happened before. I've never seen him so angry. His face didn't even look like it belonged to him anymore. It was as though I blinked and he slipped on a Halloween mask. *Boo!*

"The gun went off. He's dead."

Dead? I scratch at the back of Samuel's hand, forcing him to release me. When I throw myself into my father's lap, he tips over, his head hitting the pew with a hollow *thwunk*. His blood soaks my t-shirt. "Dad?" I slap at his cheeks, but he doesn't so much as flinch. One eyelid droops just slightly, making him appear drunk. "He's not dead," I whimper. "He just had too much whisky. I just have to get him home, tuck him into bed..."

Samuel, losing patience, picks me up, throwing me over his shoulder. I struggle, but he holds tight. I kick him over and over, but he doesn't even acknowledge it; it's as though I'm little more than a gnat. An annoyance. I'm sobbing as we leave the church, snot and tears streaming down my face, dappling the back of my stepfather's shirt. "I killed him," I wail. "I killed him!"

Samuel opens the passenger-side door of his truck, unceremoniously dropping me onto the bench seat. He grips the door, leaning in so that our faces are inches apart. "You listen to me: your daddy killed himself. He grabbed that gun, and whether it was him or you who pulled the trigger, it doesn't much matter."

I curl up into a ball on the seat, sniffling and cradling my wrist. "I'll be right back, alright?" Samuel says gently. "Stay right here." He gives my knee an affectionate squeeze. "Good boy." Opening the tailgate, he drags something heavy across the bed. The metal-on-metal whine sets my teeth on edge. When he shuffles past the truck rather than getting into the driver's side, I sit up. His right shoulder weighed down by the gas can, he climbs the stairs, dousing them in gasoline. Then he disappears inside, presumably to anoint the nave, the altar, and the tapestries. In the sunlight, the propellant seems to be made of rainbows.

Before Samuel reemerges from the church, I am gone, along with the handful of crumpled bills he keeps in the center console for emergencies. As I walk down the shoulder on highway 66, thumbing for a ride, I repeat the mantra that will protect my heart: "The Devil made me do it, the Devil made me do it, the Devil…"

Wharton, Virginia—Present Day

I like to walk. Being able to put one foot in front of the other is a gift. Someday, I imagine I won't be able to; age comes for us all, eventually. Recently, my hands have begun to cramp, my fingers twisting into Gordian knots. I had to suffer the indignity of asking one of my coworkers—a young, pimply-faced know-it-all named Dylan—for help removing a motherboard from its plastic housing. Perhaps that's why I took up this mantle of revenge now. Soon, I won't have the strength to pull the trigger.

Bird's Nest is quiet, the only sound the crunch of gravel underfoot. I walk along the shoulder, careful to keep away from the culvert; it smells foul, like garbage rotting in the sun. I'm not sure which bungalow belongs to Ama Chilton. I only have vague memories of it, and 50-some years later, it's liable to look different. With the late hour, I don't see a single person—just a cat in a window, watching me pass.

Bwoop, bwoop. A police cruiser pulls up alongside me with its turret lights blinking. The window rolls down. "Nice night," the driver drawls. He's wearing plainclothes rather than a uniform. When he rests his elbow on the window sill, the cuff of his blazer rides up, revealing a gold wristwatch.

I casually tuck my hands into my jacket, my knuckles butting against the cool metal of my pistol. "A little cold," I say.

"You live around here?"

"Just visiting. I couldn't sleep, so I thought I'd take a little walk. You know how it is: unfamiliar bed, strange sounds. I never sleep well on vacation. Good night, officer." I continue walking, hoping he'll flip a U-turn and head back into town. Instead, the cruiser keeps pace with me.

"Detective."

I pause, running my hand through my greasy hair. "What?" The nearby bungalows are dark, the curtains drawn. Had someone spotted me on the road and called the police? Worse still, had they seen me high-stepping out of the underbrush, picking nettles off of my sleeves? I must look unkempt after my tenure in the forest.

"You said 'officer.' I'm a detective." He reaches into the pocket of his blazer, and I wince, but it's just a pack of Marlboro cigarettes. He slaps the pack against his palm before opening it and selecting a cigarette. When he lights it with a cheap plastic Zippo, I catch a glimpse of his face: heavily lined, tan except around his baggy eyes, and a bristly mustache that resembles a push broom.

"My mistake," I mumble.

"Where are you staying?" Smoke pours from the detective's mouth as he speaks. He resembles a tubby dragon.

"The Great Inn."

"You're miles from there," the detective observes. "Why don't I give you a ride back into town?"

"I prefer to walk," I say, licking at my dry lips. "I appreciate the offer though, off—I mean, detective."

"I insist," the detective says coolly. "I can't have somethin' happen to you out here. The Captain'll have my head if he finds out I let a tourist wander 'round and freeze to death. Or worse."

"I'll be fine," I chuckle. "The worst thing that'll happen is that I get back too late for the continental breakfast."

The detective's jaw tightens. "Somethin' must be getting lost in translation here, 'cause I'm not fucking askin'. Get in the car."

I look up and down the quiet road, weighing my options. There aren't many of them. Either I comply, or I pull my pistol and shoot him between his beady eyes.

I'm not entirely sure I have the stomach for the latter. I'm not a cop-killer. Without a silencer, the bang will ping-pong between the rows of bungalows, waking the few people who live here during the off-season. I also can't steal his car because every officer between here and Washington D.C. will be looking for it. "Sure," I say, trying to sound congenial.

The back of the cruiser smells like stale smoke and urine. There's no barrier between the front and back seats; maybe that's only necessary in big cities with real crime. I expect Wharton's criminal underbelly is populated by bored teenagers with spray paint and drunk partygoers who drive their pontoon boats a little too fast.

The detective cranks the wheel, pointing the cruiser back toward town. There's a half-dollar-sized bald spot on the back of his head. "You're lucky I found you," the detective says, meeting my eyes in the rearview mirror. "There's an attempted murderer on the loose. Shot someone in broad daylight, right on that road you were walkin' down."

"Oh?" I am relieved to hear that the man I shot is alive. I didn't know him from Adam.

The detective drives with his wrist slung on the steering wheel. When he talks, he gesticulates with his fingers, the cigarette bobbing like a little baton. Sparks rain down upon the dash. "We also have a bit of a wildlife problem here."

I'm glad for the darkness, the streetlights few and far between. I think that if he could see me, he would be able to dissect every thought from my head. He speaks as if leading me somewhere, but the path gets more circuitous with every word. "I didn't know there were bears in Virginia, especially this far east," I comment. "Say, could I get one of those cigarettes?"

"Sure," the detective says, tossing the Zippo and pack of Marlboros into my lap. I light one, taking a drag. The smoke makes me cough. I haven't smoked in years. It was a vice I picked up after running away from home. Cigarettes were a hitchhiker's currency and a conversation-starter. "Hey man, can I bum a smoke?" got me further in life than most else.

The detective takes a long drag of his cigarette. "Wolves," he clarifies. "Usually they mind their own business. They do their thing, and we do ours. But sometimes, people rile 'em up." He flicks the remains of his cigarette out the window. "When people do that it really sticks in my craw, y'know what I mean?"

"Not really," I admit. I want to ask him if I can roll down the window. His piney cologne is giving me a headache. It's as though he bathed in it, washed his clothes in it.

"It's all about protectin' the public. Last time they got real upset, people died. Lots of 'em. There's been nothin' like that on my watch, and I want it to stay that way. They have little tussles amongst themselves, but that's alright. None of my business." He flips on the blinker, turning onto what doesn't really amount to a road.

The gravel turns to sand. Tire tracks are the only evidence that cars belong here. The headlights bob, and in the distance, I catch a glimpse of the dark, shifting void that is the ocean. We creep past the remnants of a sand fence: narrow cedar slats, inches apart, held together by braided wire. A wind-battered metal sign reads: "Over Sand Vehicle Zone."

"This isn't the way to town," I murmur. I give the door handle a tug, but it doesn't budge. The doors are locked. The gun is a lead weight in my pocket, but I'm too dithery to retrieve it. If this is just an innocent detour and I overreact, I'm finished.

"No," the detective replies, "it's not." He stops the car, putting it in park. "Mr. Fairbanks, I take my job very seriously. I'm a peacekeeper. Simple as that. You're making it awfully hard to keep the fuckin' peace."

"How do you know my na—"

When he turns to look at me, his service weapon is in his hand. He squeezes the trigger before I can finish my sentence, and the car's interior seems to explode. It feels as though I've been punched in the chest, and I slam back against the seat. Warmth pools in my lap, but I can't seem to move my head to look at the damage. I expect to feel pain, but there is none.

The detective stares at me for a long moment before tucking his gun back into the shoulder holster beneath his blazer. "It's nothin' personal," he says, reaching for the burning cigarette still loosely held between my middle and ring fingers. The last thing I see is the filter ignite as he takes a drag—my own circle of hell.

CHAPTER 24
(HUNTER)

————◁◆▷————

I wake to the sun pouring through the blinds; stripes of sunlight and shadow paint a pattern upon the bedspread. Ghost unapologetically walks across my midsection to find the warmest sunbeam to laze in. When I sit up, I think that I can convince myself it was all a bad dream. The bedroom looks just as it did when I left the house the morning Asher was born. Even the mug I'd left on the bedside table is still there, the tea tag dangling over the rim. However, when I'd left, the bed didn't have a dirt-covered man dozing in it.

Angus stirs, rubbing at his sleep-crusted eyes with his knuckles. I lean over to kiss him. He still smells like the outdoors, the very tip of his nose reddened by the cold. "There's dirt in the bed," I observe.

"Mm," Angus deadpans. "I think you let a dog in here."

"I'm going to take a shower," I snicker, swatting at his muscular arm. Naked, I pad across the room to the en-suite bathroom. I twist on the tap, sticking my fingers amidst the stream to test the temperature.

When it warms, I step inside the cubicle. It feels good to pick off all of the cruddy adhesive left on my inner elbows, the back of my hand. Angus steps into the cubicle just as I lather my hair, his lips pressing against my stubbly neck.

I close my eyes as soapy water dribbles down my forehead. "This still feels like a dream," he murmurs. "That any second I'll wake up, and I'll find myself back at your bedside."

"I'm home," I assure him. When I lean back against his unyielding body, his cock stirs. He reaches for the bar of soap on the shelf, running it over the flat plane of my belly.

"*We're* home," Angus amends. He sensuously cleans my body from head to toe. It's as though he has to touch every inch of me, to assure himself I'm corporeal rather than a figment of his imagination. When he is done, I take the sudsy bar of soap from his hand.

I turn in his arms so that I can scrub his chest. He watches me through half-lidded eyes, his nostrils flaring as my soapy hands descend to his waist and then, lower still. He is already impossibly hard, his cock standing at attention. When I touch it, he groans. "Tease!"

"I have no intention of teasing you," I chuckle, running the pad of my thumb over the slit. Being wolfish has heightened my desire tenfold; I want to devour him, in every conceivable way.

"Angus?" Candy calls, knocking on the closed bathroom door. "I heard the shower—is that you?"

Angus sighs, grinding the heels of his hands into his eye sockets. "Yeah!" he finally calls. "I'll be out in

a minute." He bites at his lip. "Actually, make that five."
Wordlessly, he grasps a fistful of my hair, pushing me
back against the cool linoleum wall. He does not have
to be gentle, and I don't want him to be.

Candy is pacing the kitchen when we finally
emerge with damp hair and rosy cheeks. "Hunter!" she
gasps, tears brimming in her eyes. She throws her arms
around my neck. "You're—" A sob bubbles out of her.

"I'm home," I finish for her. The last week must
have been agonizing for her. We spent so much of
our adolescence in the hospital, watching our mother
wither beneath an I.V. pole. Her death was a series
of little dips: vomiting up blood, swelling limbs, confused questions that broke our hearts. "Whose kids are
these?" she'd ask our father, scooting her chair away
as though we carried the plague. When she was lucid,
we'd play rounds of Go Fish until she nodded off, chin
to chest. Candy had her homecoming dance photos
taken in the oncology ward.

"Oh my god," she sobs into my ear. "Haley said
you'd run off. She's been out looking for you for hours.
Mrs. Campbell too."

"I should have called," Angus murmurs apologetically. "I left my phone in the hospital. When we came
home, you were asleep—we didn't want to wake you."

Candy finally releases me, tucking her hair behind
her ears. "There was a note on the door," she sniffles,
tapping her fingers upon a folded-up piece of paper on
the countertop. "I think you need to see it."

Angus unfolds it, reading aloud: "'Meet me at the
mushrooms.'" He presses his lips together, clearly
troubled by it. "There's no signature."

"The mushrooms?" Candy asks. I don't know what the cryptic message means either.

"Leigh's gravesite."

♦ ♦ ♦

It takes an hour to hike to the place where Angus buried her. Most of it is uphill, and I huff and puff, my breath coming out as vapor. It's colder here; the canopy only allows a bit of sunlight to reach the leaf litter. When we start to see the white caps of wild mushrooms amidst the foliage, I expect we are close. "Did you know that mushrooms talk to each other?" I ask. "Through their mycelium."

Angus doesn't seem to hear me. He's looking at something in the distance—sunlight bouncing off of a reflective surface. It's a police cruiser, with Wharton Sheriff's Office emblazoned upon the door. "How did that get here?" I whisper. The underbrush is dense, and it is difficult to traverse even on foot.

"Deer trails," Angus murmurs. "They are all over this area."

The driver's side door of the cruiser swings open as we approach, and Detective Acker clambers out. "Mr. Chilton, Mr. Bailey," he says, by way of greeting. He doesn't seem particularly surprised to see me up and about.

Angus approaches slowly, his hands in his pockets. "Detective." His voice is preternaturally even. There's a hole dug amidst the mushrooms, a long-handled spade propped against a maple tree. At the bottom of the hole, I spot the corner of a dirty blue tarp poking through the freshly turned soil.

"Oh Jesus," I groan, turning away. "Is that—?" *Leigh*.

Even though it is cold, Detective Acker's brow is glossy with sweat. "I have a gift for you, Mr. Chilton."

"And it isn't even my birthday." Angus warily looks around the surrounding forest, his nostrils flaring. But there's nothing to see, nor smell. Not for miles.

"I assure you, I came alone," the detective says. "But you can smell that, can't you?" He shuts the driver's side door, lumbering toward the back of the vehicle. Without fanfare, he opens the trunk with a key. The smell of death wafts out.

Angus and I move closer. Inside the trunk, a dead man lays on his side, his knees drawn up to his chest. There's a bullet hole between his sightless eyes, a tiny trickle of blood tracing the shape of his nose. He must be in his late sixties, his face well-lined and his hair thinning; dirt is packed into every wrinkle, making them appear impossibly deep. His clothes are soiled, the smell of body odor seemingly baked into the fabric. While I've never seen him before, there's something oddly familiar about him. "Here lies Henry Fairbanks," the detective intones, as though delivering a eulogy. "Ashes to ashes, and dust to fuckin' dust."

"Who is that?" I ask, pinching my nostrils shut. I feel as though I can *taste* him. It takes everything in me not to vomit.

"He's the man who shot you," Angus murmurs. "He's Haley's uncle." That's why he looks familiar. They have the same round, hazel eyes and ashy tones in their hair.

The detective leans in to grab the man beneath the arms, heaving him upright. "Grab his feet, would you?" he grunts.

Mutely, Angus does as the detective asks. Together, they shuffle toward the hole, dropping the man in. A cloud of dirt wafts into the air. Angus wipes his hands on his jeans. "What is this?"

"I told you: this is a gift," Detective Acker says. "What comes next will require a bit o' quid pro quo, if you catch my drift."

"I'm listening," Angus says, looking down into the deep hole.

"I know what you are," Detective Acker says, fishing a pack of cigarettes out of his blazer. He takes his time lighting it, cupping his hand around the tip to keep the flame from sputtering out. "Just like my father and his father before him. It's obvious, if you have half a brain. Lucky for you: most Whartonites don't. I turn the other cheek when y'all have your spats, because it doesn't fuckin' concern me. But I'm an old man now. I don't have the bandwidth to be fieldin' calls from Portland fuckin' P.D."

Angus' face is impassive. "I didn't have anything to do with the Nedry murder."

"Sure," the detective says, smoke spewing out of his mouth. "But you do know why they can't locate James Volkov."

Angus just shrugs.

Detective Acker taps a bit of ash off the end of his cigarette. "I do have one more lie in me. So, if y'all get out of town, I'll make sure Portland doesn't come sniffin' around again. And by 'y'all' I mean *you fuckin' all*. I don't want to see another wolf in this county. That includes Ama Chilton."

"If we don't?" I ask. I feel as though I'm standing on a cliff, about to get pushed off. Wharton is my home.

"Let's say you decided to kill me right here," the detective says, "and bury me right on top of our new friend here. An email will go out to Portland P.D., CC'ing my department heads in—" he checks his wristwatch "—ninety-three minutes, with information about your whereabouts; known accomplices, including your grandmother; and the coordinates for this gravesite. You'll be arrested or dead before the sun goes down, and that little baby will be in foster care."

Angus' blue eye settles on me. He licks at his dry lips. "Hunter has lived here his entire life. He's a pillar of this community. His mother is buried in the cemetery. We can't just leave, we—"

"Yes, we can," I interrupt. "We can just leave. Wharton is just a place. You and the others are my family, and my home is wherever you are. Besides," I chuckle, to keep from weeping, "the café already has wheels."

III. January

EPILOGUE
(ANGUS)

---◁◆▷---

E bb and Flow 2 Go is parked in the shadow of Paul Bunyan's lumbering statue. Despite the freezing temperatures in Bangor, the line of would-be patrons meanders through the park, spilling out onto Main Street. While I can't readily see Hunter, I can hear him: "Peppermint mocha for Jay!" he calls.

I open the door, climbing inside the Westfalia bus. I'm nearly bowled over by Matias, the recent hire. His apron strings have come untied, and there's a bit of what I think is caramel drizzle on his cheek. Haley expertly skirts around the frazzled barista to retrieve the milk frother. When she spots me, she frowns. "Don't you have somewhere to be?"

Hunter leans out the window, handing the mocha to a tall man in a leather jacket and tightly wrapped pagri, a Joe Hill paperback tucked under his arm. "Enjoy!" When he spots me, his face splits into a grin.

"Aren't you a little late for something?" I ask, quirking an eyebrow. I try to look stern.

He pales. "I lost track of time. We've been so busy."

Haley grabs his arm, steering him toward me. "Go, go. Matias and I've got this. Right, Matty?" Matias looks a little green at the prospect, but he nods.

Hunter looks unconvinced. "C'mon," I badger him, "this will take five minutes, then we can come right back."

"Over my dead body. Please go enjoy your honeymoon," Haley says over her shoulder, already punching the next order into the register. "Matty, I need a flat white!" Matias hustles to pull a shot of ristretto.

Hunter pulls off his apron, hanging it on the hook. He rolls down the sleeves of his dress shirt, which are hopelessly wrinkled. "I'm sorry," he says, shrugging on his suit jacket. "I really did lose track of time."

I offer him my elbow, kissing the corner of his mouth. "It can't start without us," I assure him.

Hunter picks a bit of imaginary fuzz off my sleeve. "You clean up nice."

Together, we rush across the grassy park to the arbor and chairs. Our guests are waiting in their seats: Ama, Toby with baby Asher, and Alexandre.

Candy stands at the outset of the short aisle, her heels sinking into the soft earth. She reaches for her brother's hand. "Imagine being late to your own wedding because you had to make a fucking cappuccino! *Honestly!*"

"I was short-staffed," Hunter chuckles as I fly past them. "Most of them took off to go to a wedding."

The officiant sniffs disapprovingly as I scramble to stand beside him. "Sorry!" I whisper. "Let's begin." Just as the music starts—an instrumental version of some pop song I don't recognize—a snowflake alights on the officiant's shoulder. More follow, mottling the aisle. Hunter stops midway down the aisle, looking up with wonder. "Angus," he says, "Angus ... it's snowing."

THE END.

Book Club Questions

◁◆▷

1. Was Hunter's ultimatum fair?
2. Henry is driven to hunt in order to assuage his guilt. Why was Haley his target?
3. Was Angus' apology in the hospital enough, or should Hunter have stood his ground?
4. Angus recalls a memory of Ama and Flora on the phone, discussing the impending execution of Freddy Parnell. How did his death—and the pack's involvement—compare to Leigh's?
5. The pack goes on a deer hunt in nearly every Wolves of Wharton book to (1) exemplify the pack's current dynamic or (2) exacerbate conflict. What did you learn from Angus and Hunter's first hunt together?
6. Hunter is suffering from post-traumatic stress. Angus is too, but his symptoms are less typical. What are they?
7. Ama is the only character to appear—or be mentioned in—every Wolves of Wharton Book. What characteristics does she embody?

8. Henry doesn't get a complete villain arc; like many villains, he doesn't learn a lesson. What do you think he meant by the following: "The last thing I see is the [cigarette] filter ignite as he takes a drag—my own circle of hell"? What do you think hell looks like for him?

9. Leigh is a complicated figure, especially in Hunter's dreams/hallucinations. She describes herself as the "Ghost of Christmas Past." In *A Christmas Carol*, that particular ghost shows Scrooge his mistakes and ultimately helped to perpetuate change. Did Leigh do this for Hunter? Why or why not?

10. As Angus says, most of what occurs is because he made a mistake keeping James alive. How would the story be different if he hadn't? Were Angus and Hunter destined to be together, or were they, as Angus feared, trauma bonded?

ABOUT THE AUTHOR
BEAU LAKE

—◁◆▷—

B eau Lake is a tattooed, rainbow -haired, queer romance writer skulking around the mountains of Virginia. She is very happily married and lives with a menagerie of children (3), dogs (2), and plants.

Her current hobbies include digital art, social/animal activism, and screaming into the void. Mostly the latter. Other favorite activities include listening to true crime podcasts, staring at empty Word documents while having existential crises, and asking herself "What Would Stephen King Do?"

Beau writes both traditional and horror/supernatural LGBTQIA romance. Werewolves are her favorite because they have sharp teeth and even sharper personalities.

Some of her published work includes the well-received DC Pride series, co-written with Tatum West

(Proud, Out, and The Space Between Us). The Wolves of Wharton is her first paranormal romance series, with more to come!

She can be found online via Facebook, Twitter, TikTok or at beaulakebooks.com. She loves talking with readers and can be reached at authorbeaulake@gmail.com.

----◁◆▷----

OTHER BOOKS

Co-authored w/ Tatum West:
Proud, Out, The Space Between Us

BY BEAU LAKE:

The Beast Beside Me
The Beast Within Me
Taming the Beast
The Beast After Me
Charming the Beast

4 Horsemen Publications

Romance

Ann Shepphird
The War Council

Emily Bunney
All or Nothing
All the Way
All Night Long
All She Needs
Having it All
All at Once
All Together

All for Her
Lynn Chantale
The Baker's Touch
Blind Secrets

Mimi Francis
Private Lives
Second Chances
Run Away Home
The Professor

Fantasy & Paranormal Romance

Beau Lake
The Beast Beside Me
The Beast Within Me
The Beast After Me
The Beast Like Me
An Eye for Emeralds
Swimming in Sapphires
Pining for Pearls

D. Lambert
To Walk into the Sands
Rydan
Northlander
Esparan
King
Traitor
His Last Name

YOUNG ADULT FANTASY

4HorsemenPublications.com